THE DEMON IN THE DEN

COURTNEY MCFARLIN

For My Love. Thank you for your inspiration, dedication, and support.

$\mathcal{Y}$ou know how a lot of cat owners wish they could talk to their cats? I had always dreamed that maybe someday it would be possible, and imagined how incredible it would be. What I forgot to factor in was that my cat, Bernie, who was apparently more than just a simple cat, loved waking me up early. When all I could hear were meows, it was easy enough to toss the covers over my head and grab a few more minutes of sleep. Now, though? Let's just say it was a little more difficult.

"Hey. You. Get. Up. Now," Bernie said, his voice booming into my ear from his position on my pillow as he enunciated each word.

"Just five more minutes. We were up late last night talking."

"I'm hungry."

"You're always hungry," I said, flinging off the covers as dramatically as possible and heaving myself to my feet. "I thought cats were supposed to sleep like sixteen or eighteen hours a day."

I heard Bernie's little black feet hit the wooden floor with a loud thump as he followed me, tail held high.

"I think we've established I'm not your average cat."

"Ain't that the truth?"

"I heard that."

"I wasn't whispering."

He brushed my leg as he passed me, jogging into the kitchen. My brain finally caught up with the rest of me and I yawned, running a hand through my mop of hair. A few weeks ago, I'd suddenly developed the ability to understand my cat, thanks in part to a strange ghost named Edward Davis, who preferred to be called Ned. Yeah, I talk to ghosts and cats. I'm a real draw at parties. Not.

Since then, Bernie and I had gone through what he liked to call a transition period of working out our new pecking order. Other than the whole talking thing, not much had changed. He still ran the house with an iron paw, but on the plus side, I could now understand what he meant, instead of guessing. According to Ned, Bernie was much more than a cat, but he either didn't know, or wasn't willing to share, what that meant. After meeting Ned, either of those options was entirely possible.

"What can I fix you this morning?" I asked, looking longingly at the coffeemaker.

Cats before coffee. A great new rule we're following. Yay. That and no more actual cat food. Bernie preferred the human grade stuff now, like canned chicken, salmon, and tuna. Honestly, I didn't blame him.

"Salmon, please. And plenty of it."

I dished up his food and set it on the counter for him before adding a scoop of coffee grounds into my filter. Just to be on the safe side, I added another scoop. It couldn't hurt, right?

I grabbed my phone and paged through my notifications while I waited for the coffee to brew. No texts, no calls. I sighed as I leaned back against the counter. I ran an interior design and home staging company, and things had slowed down lately. I'd finished my latest job of decorating the newly renovated suites at a historic hotel right before the local annual motorcycle rally.

That rally doubled the population of our tiny state for two weeks, and while it was huge for our businesses, it made getting around nearly impossible. Maybe things would pick up now that it was over. I tapped my fingers on the counter while I watched the coffee drip into the pot. Was it me or was it dripping slower?

"Are you going to stare at that until it's done?"

"Maybe. Sorry, I'm grouchy this morning," I said, shaking my head. "I just feel out of sorts. I need to work on something."

"If you're that bored, see if Logan needs any help," Bernie said before running a paw over his ear.

Logan was my cousin, but we were so close in age he felt more like a brother. An annoying older brother who delighted in teasing me. A few weeks ago, he'd been poisoned and nearly died, but he'd healed fast and was back working at the construction company our fathers had founded.

"I guess I could. Zane's supposed to be back in town tomorrow, too. It seems like he's been gone forever."

Zane Matthews was my boyfriend, a fact that never failed to send a little zip down my spine. The handsome New Yorker with long dark hair and icy blue eyes had claimed my heart, and even though it had been rough, he accepted who I was and what I could do. Adding the fact that I could now hear Bernie hadn't even phased him. He'd started his own security business when he moved here a few months ago, and it had really taken off. He'd been in Las Vegas for the past week, attending a security conference, and I missed him terribly.

"Your coffee's done," Bernie said, pausing his cleanup routine.

"Finally," I said, grabbing my cup and filling it to the brim.

A few sips later, I felt human and a lot less cranky. I knew it was normal for my business to go through high and low periods. Typically, when this happened, I'd head to auctions in other states to stock up on antiques. My storage unit was almost cleaned out, thanks to the project at the hotel, which meant I finally had room to add a few more pieces.

"Do you think we should go out of town? We could hit up a few estate auctions."

Bernie shot me a look, his emerald eyes gleaming as the morning sun streamed into the kitchen.

"I don't think that will be necessary."

I narrowed my eyes as I took another sip. I had a feeling he knew more than he was telling me. I opened my mouth to reply when my phone rang. Bernie smirked as he straightened and wrapped his tail around his feet. He might be more than a cat, but to me, he'd always be my mini-panther.

"Sullivan Staging, this is Brynn."

"This is Stephen Graff. You were recommended to me by Bob Tremaine."

My heart rate sped up. Bob, a local realtor, knew of my reputation as being more than a simple home stager. He'd hired me to help him with a ghost problem at a Victorian home that turned into a murder investigation.

"Yes. Are you looking for some help to stage your home for sale?"

He barked out a laugh that made Bernie's ears swivel and the cat sidled closer to me, putting his head near the receiver.

"Not exactly. I'm hosting a family event in a few days and I need some professional help. I was told you also do interior design. Is that correct?"

"It is. Typically, most of my work is for remodels, rather than onetime events. I'm not sure..."

"Great. You've got the job. I need you to be here to look at the project and you'll need to start immediately. I live at 333 Honeysuckle Court, in the canyon. See you in one hour."

He ended the call, leaving me staring at the phone with my mouth open. I turned to look at Bernie, whose whiskers were quirked up in amusement.

"Well, I guess he told you. Better get a move on. See, now you don't have to worry about not having anything to do."

He jumped down from the counter and headed into the living room, leaving me in the kitchen, still uncertain of what had just happened.

"But I didn't say I'd take the job," I said, muttering to myself as I went back to my bedroom to get ready for the day. "Staging a house for a family event?"

Bernie popped his head around the corner as I grabbed a pair of jeans and a shirt.

"You know what they say about people who talk to themselves?"

"Probably the same thing they say about people who talk to cats. Seriously, though. This is kind of weird request."

"Eh, he's a rich guy who's probably never heard no. You can always turn him down in person," Bernie said, hopping on the bed and laying on my tee before I could put it on.

"Hey, I'm wearing that today."

"Yes, I realize that. I'm simply making sure you look your best."

I rolled my eyes as I brushed his black fur off the blue fabric before pulling it on over my head.

"I wonder if there's something more to his request. It just seems odd somehow. He talked to Bob and Bob knows about my, um, abilities. How do you know he's rich?"

"He lives in the canyon. You won't know till you go," Bernie said, jumping down and heading out of my room. "Hurry. It takes at least a half an hour to get there. I'm going with you, of course."

"Of course," I said, as I wrestled my curly hair into submission.

It was a losing battle, but I finally got it into an approximation of a ponytail. Good enough. I slapped on some mascara and lip gloss before heading back into the living room, where I found Bernie waiting in his carrier, moving his claws in and out of the plush lining.

"Finally. Let's go."

"How am I going to explain that I'm bringing my cat to this impromptu meeting?" I asked as I opened the door and made sure it was locked before heading down the sidewalk.

Bernie sighed loudly.

"This isn't my first rodeo. He won't even know I'm there. Honestly, I don't know why we bother with this carrier business. I should be free like God intended cats to be."

"Well, you're small and fragile and I want nothing to happen to you," I said, climbing in and putting his bag on the seat next to me. "I care about you, buddy."

He let out a little chirp that made me smile, remembering when that was his primary way of communicating. I was still thrilled he made those noises every once in a while.

"Back at you," he said, getting comfortable as I turned on the ignition. "Where are we going for lunch?"

"You just had breakfast."

"Yes, and now I'm ready to think about lunch. I'd like some bacon."

I turned up the music and headed onto the highway that would link up with the scenic canyon road, grateful traffic was back to its usual levels. I live in Gilded City, a small town just a few miles from the historic town of Deadwood, South Dakota. While tourists were a daily occurrence, especially in summer, the sheer amount of people who crammed into town for the rally slowed everything to a crawl.

I loved the area, especially since my main calling was fixing up old houses and helping ghosts, both of which were prevalent. I'd grown up here, and even though I thought of leaving when I was struggling through high school, I was glad I still called the place home. There was nothing like the fresh scent of the pine trees that gave the Black Hills their name, and the wide open spaces were amazing.

I'd never heard of Stephen Graff, but from what I could gather from his call, he was a person used to getting his way. I wasn't sure what I was about to run into, but it was better than sitting at home, wondering what to do with myself.

"Tell you what, Bern. We'll go see this guy, and if the project looks promising, we'll take it. After that, I'll take you to lunch at Jill's. Sound good?"

He nodded before snapping his head around to look out the window. We'd just passed a mountain goat clinging to the side of a hill, and his hunter instincts were fully engaged. I smiled as I turned onto the canyon road.

2

*a*fter winding through the canyon, squinting at signs as I drove past, I finally found 333 Honeysuckle Court. A massive black iron gate blocked the private driveway, and I glanced over at Bernie before pulling up next to the intercom system on the side of the road. As I rolled my window down, the mechanism buzzed, and the gate swung open slowly. I guess they were expecting me.

I kept my window down, appreciating the crisp air as I followed the winding driveway. Most homes in this area made do with dirt or gravel for their roads, but this guy had apparently gone all out and paved the entire surface with blacktop. I let out a low whistle as we rounded the corner and the house came into view.

"Looks like you were right, Bern. This guy definitely isn't hurting."

"I'm always right," Bernie said, tempering his words with a slow blink.

I parked under a massive overhang and ruffled his fur before turning off my car. The exterior of the house was completely covered in natural stone, and it looked bigger than a hotel. I couldn't imagine rattling around in a place like this, but I guess to each their own, right?

"Ready for this?"

"Just let me out and I'll take it from there."

Bernie sprang across my lap and was out my window before I could blink.

"Hey!"

There was no response and I couldn't see him anymore. I shook my head as I unbuckled my seat belt and got out.

The front door was wide enough for a marching band to pass through it, and I felt even shorter than usual as I pressed the bell on the door. It swung open, revealing a man in a black suit. His immaculate white hair was styled into an astonishing pompadour that wouldn't have been out of place at an Elvis impersonator's reunion.

"Right this way, Miss."

I bit my tongue, grateful I hadn't accidentally addressed him as Mr. Graff. This guy had a butler! In South Dakota, of all places. I followed behind, trying to keep up with the sprightly older man as he led me down a long hallway. Briefly, I wondered if there was etiquette for interacting with a butler. Were you supposed to ignore them? Tip them?

I skidded on the polished floor as he came to a sudden halt in front of a French door. The rich, mahogany wood gleamed, even in the low light of the hallway, and my fingers itched to touch it.

He tapped on the door and I heard a gruff voice I recognized as belonging to Mr. Graff bark out an order.

"Enter."

The butler swung the door open and stepped aside to allow me to pass. I smiled at him as I entered the room, wondering where on earth Bernie had gone. Was he pulling an invisible act? If he was, I hoped he'd hustle his little furry butt through the door before it closed.

"You're early, Miss Sullivan. An admirable trait."

"Thank you," I said as I looked around the office.

Its paneled shelves and myriad of books would have made my friend Sophie Ryman salivate. She ran the Deadwood Public Library and was the only person I knew who loved books more than I did. I wondered if they were for show, or well loved, before finally dragging my gaze to the man sitting behind the desk.

His pale face was lined heavily. He didn't look like a man who smiled much. His hair was steel gray, slicked back off his prominent forehead. I supposed in his youth he would have been handsome, but he gave off an overbearing air of displeasure that hung around him like a cloud.

I stuck my hand across his desk and he looked at it in surprise before grasping it. His handshake was solid, and I reluctantly put a check mark on the positive side of my mental assessment of him. My dad always said you can tell a lot about a person from their hand-shake, and he was rarely wrong.

"Please take a seat," he said, leaning back in his chair.

I sat in the burgundy leather chair across from his desk and slipped a little on the slick surface, feeling absurdly like a child as I got settled. He wove his fingers together across his narrow frame and eyed me impassively. I took the bull by the horns and blurted out what I was thinking.

"Thank you for inviting me to your impressive home, but I'm still not sure how we can work together. As I was saying when you called, I rarely do staging for events."

He waved an elegant hand, dismissing my concerns, before looking me in the eye.

"Money isn't an object. You'll be well compensated for your services. I realize this may be something different from your usual purview, but it's essential that I have a professional help me with these preparations."

"I don't mean to appear rude, but don't you have staff who could assist you? I mean, you have a butler, so I assume you have other staff."

I trailed off, watching as a form appeared behind Stephen Graff's chair. The shape solidified into a man wearing an old-fashioned three-piece-suit, complete with boutonniere. He gave me an unfriendly look as he started pacing back and forth. Well, this was interesting.

"I have staff, but none that are capable of what you can do. I trust Bob. He's an old family friend. When I mentioned needing someone with a keen eye for design, he instantly recommended you. This house was built in the late 1880s and I must have someone who understands old homes do the work."

This guy would not take no for an answer. The ghost behind him curled his lip into a sneer as he looked at me. From his features, I guessed he was Stephen's father, or possibly grandfather. I was intrigued, despite my misgivings about this project.

"You said you are holding a family event in a few days. What do you want changed with the place in that short time frame?"

His face relaxed, as if he felt me bending to his will.

"There have been several renovations done to the home over that time period," he said, a shadow crossing over his face. "I would like this room and the public rooms arranged as they used to be when it was first built. I have pictures you can work from, but of course, you will be allowed some design license to do as you see fit."

He slid a binder across the polished surface of his desk towards me and I took it, cracking open the cover, studying the pictures to get a sense of what he was looking for.

"Do you want anything painted? It will be very difficult to get the correct colors mixed and applied in just a few days."

The album was fascinating at first glance. It was full of pictures of the Golden Age, reminding me of my ghostly friend, Charles Thurgood. I needed to visit him and see if he knew this family.

"No, there's no need for that. I simply want to replace the modern furniture with the antique pieces I have stored in the attic. I will rely on you to make sure everything is as it was in those photos."

"And you want this done in two days?" I asked, closing the binder so I could look at him. "I'm not sure that will be possible. I don't want to set expectations too high."

I didn't fully understand why he wanted to do this, but I definitely wanted to know more. I particularly wanted to know more about the ghost who was currently boring holes into Stephen's back with an angry glare. If that meant taking on this project, then I would try it, even against my better judgment.

"You'll get it done. It will mean long hours and I would like you to start immediately. As I mentioned, you will be well compensated for your time. Five thousand per day, to be paid when you complete the work."

My tongue tripped over itself as I did the math. Ten thousand dollars to rearrange some furniture and match the decor to the pictures? What on earth?

"Mr. Graff, that seems excessive. I typically charge a flat retainer and then bill by the hour, plus any materials I provide."

He waved away my concerns again, as the ghost switched his glowering eyes to me. A shiver went down my back as we made eye contact, and I nodded at him. The ghost's eyes flew open, startled, and he poofed out of sight.

"The amount I gave seems fair to me. Reginald will see you to the attic so you can inspect the furniture. If anything cannot be used, I will happily pay for replacements, if you have something that is appropriate on hand."

"I guess I could source a few pieces from local dealers, but I want to warn you, it might not be possible."

Why would anyone would pay ten thousand dollars to have their house rearranged for a family reunion? But then again, who was I to judge? I could see why Graff was someone who always got his way. He simply refused to entertain any idea that someone would say no.

"I'm confident you will fulfill your end of the arrangement. I have business in town, but Reginald will assist you in whatever you need. Meals will be provided while you work, so you won't have to leave the premises. My family members will arrive in two days, but everything must be finished by Thursday at seven in the evening. I will be gone tomorrow, so you can focus on this room then. The dining room, den, and the entrance will be your priorities."

He pushed a button on his desk phone and gave me a dismissing nod. I turned to see the door open behind me, and the butler with the amazing hair was standing there, smiling at me. I guess I had a job, even if I didn't want it.

"Right this way, miss," Reginald said, beckoning me to follow him.

I glanced back at Stephen Graff, but it was as if I'd ceased to exist. His head was bent as he studied a paper on his desk and he didn't acknowledge me as I stood to follow the butler. This day was turning out to be one of my strangest yet, and that was saying something.

I exited the office and hustled to catch up to Reginald, hoping he'd be a little more talkative than his boss. He gave me a sharp nod as I pulled alongside and slowed his pace a little.

"Sorry, I'm used to rushing. I'll moderate my steps," he said.

"I'm just short. I'm used to catching up. Have you worked here for a long time?" I asked, trying not to pant as I promised myself that one of these days I'd get my rear end to the gym and work on my cardio.

"I've been with the family for fifty years," he said. "And my father served for seventy years before that."

"Wow, that's impressive. I can't imagine working in one place for that long. Are there other people on staff here?"

"Yes, there's my wife Mimi. She serves as the housekeeper and cook, and then we have a few girls who help her clean occasionally."

"Oh, that's wonderful that you can work together."

"Yes, the Graffs have always been excellent employers."

I was just about to ask him about the former Mr. Graff to see if my hunch was right, that the ghost I'd seen was related to Stephen, but he came to a sudden stop in front of a door. He took a ring of keys out of his pocket and opened it, flipping on a light switch that illuminated a steep set of stairs.

"Wow, that's the attic access?"

"Yes. Don't worry, we have a larger stairwell at the back of the house that is wide enough for moving furniture. This one was closer to the office. I was briefed this morning on your duties, and will be happy to help move the heavier pieces."

My lips quirked at Stephen Graff's high-handedness. I'd put money that he'd told his butler I'd be doing the work before he even asked me. I glanced at Reginald, wondering how a man who was obviously in his seventies was going to move heavy furniture, but I didn't want to offend him.

"I have a few people I can tap to help with any large pieces. I'm sure you have your own duties you'll need to attend to."

Reginald flashed a smile, showing a set of startlingly white teeth.

"Much appreciated, miss. I hadn't expected you to be so small and I'll admit, I was wondering how this was going to work. I have a few things I need to do, and if it doesn't seem too presumptuous, I would recommend going through everything first before you decide what you'll need to bring down. We can come up with a plan once you've seen it all. Less work that way."

I grinned at him, appreciating his attitude. I'd never worked with a butler before, but I sensed we were going to become friends during my short time here.

"That sounds like an excellent idea. Is there anything I should know before I head up there?"

His friendly face darkened, and he opened his mouth before closing it abruptly and turning away.

"Just watch yourself, miss. If you need me, there are intercom buttons set-up in every room, even up there. They buzz down to the kitchen."

It was like being in my very own episode of Downton Abbey, and I was secretly thrilled, even though I wondered what he'd thought of saying before he changed his mind.

"Excellent. Thank you, Reginald. It might take me a few hours to go through everything up there."

"Splendid. Mimi will have lunch ready in two hours. I'll call you via the intercom when it's ready."

He nodded and turned, walking back down the hallway quickly. I eyed the narrow stairs and took a deep breath. What was I going to find up there? The wooden steps creaked a little as I walked, and I grabbed the railing for support as I reached the top.

The expansive space took my breath away. I'd expected a dark, dusty attic, but this was incredible. Large mullioned windows allowed plenty of light to stream into the space, making it seem almost cheerful. There wasn't any dust in sight and I wondered who kept everything clean. By the time you'd finish dusting, you'd have to start all over again.

"I knew you'd take the job," Bernie said from behind me.

I whipped around to see my mischievous black cat stretched out on an antique chaise lounge, sunning like he didn't have a care in the world.

"How did you?"

"Never mind that. We need to talk."

3

*W*hile I was used to Bernie suddenly showing up places, something he'd done since he joined our family when I was a little girl, seeing him lounging in the attic, threw me for a loop. I put the photo album down next to him on the chaise and crossed my arms, wondering if he'd ever stop surprising me. Knowing him, I already knew the answer to that question.

"Okay. Do you mean, beyond the fact I somehow feel like I got roped into an impossible job I don't know how to complete on time?"

Bernie stretched, his little toes digging into the velour fabric of the chaise, and yawned widely before looking at me.

"This was all meant to happen. I sense there's something more going on here than a simple family reunion," he said, passing a paw around an ear as he groomed his fur.

"You're telling me. What about the ghost in the office?"

His paw stopped in mid-swipe and his adorable pink tongue stuck out a little as he goggled at me. He might be more than a simple cat, but it was in moments like this that I couldn't resist booping him on the nose. He quickly retracted his tongue and gave me a dirty look.

"What do you mean?"

"I thought you came into the office with me. Where were you?"

15

"Never mind that," he said, straightening. "What ghost?"

"Well, there was an older man who appeared behind Stephen when he was talking. They looked quite a lot alike, so I'm guessing whoever it was had to be a Graff. He had the nastiest expression on his face, one that seems familiar to the family. Once he made eye contact with me, he poofed away."

"Interesting," Bernie said, digging his claws into the fabric again.

I gently disengaged his claws, picked him up and put him on my lap as I brushed his fur off the velour. He snuggled into my chest and started kneading my thigh.

"I may need to use this piece downstairs, so let's not shred it. By the way, I've got two days and a smidge longer to complete this job, and I don't know how I'm going to make it happen. I need to get to work."

Bernie leaned against me, rumbling out a purr as I described the ghost I'd seen in more detail and what I was expected to do for this job. The combination of a snuggly cat, a comfortable chair, and warm sunlight was making my eyes heavy, so I stood and started walking around, carrying Bernie against my shoulder.

"I sensed another ghost, but not the one you saw. This place is crawling with many interesting things. The one I saw is a younger woman, and she was dressed similarly to the ghost you saw. We'll need to do some research."

"Unless you know how to clone me, unfortunately, our research is going to wait. My first task is to sort through these things and organize them by room. I've got the photos to help, but this is going to be an arduous task. I can feel it."

He squiggled in my arms, and I let him down. He immediately started smoothing the fur I'd rumpled.

"Fine. I'll see what I can learn while you do your thing up here. I'm sensing many uncovered mysteries are lurking around this place."

"Sorry, I won't be able to take you to Jill's today, bud. Maybe we can go once this is all done."

He paused mid-step and gave me his patented starving cat look. I swear he could collapse his sides and appear like he hadn't eaten in weeks.

"I guess that's fine. I'll just photosynthesize like a plant or something."

I rolled my eyes as I picked up the photo album and sat back down to go through it.

"Reginald, that's the butler, says his wife is the cook here. Meals will be provided while we're working, and I'll make sure you get something to eat. Besides, you just ate an entire can of salmon."

He put his nose up in the air and swished his tail back and forth indignantly.

"Mere morsels. I require more than the average cat."

"Yeah, yeah. I'll save you some of my lunch."

He sniffed loudly before walking off, tail held high. I paged through the pictures, thinking about a game plan. It would be all too easy to get overwhelmed, so I needed to be organized. Going room by room seemed like the best bet. Graff mentioned starting in the dining room, den, and entry way, so I picked the entrance as the easiest one to knock out first.

I zeroed in the pictures that corresponded to that room, and slid them out of their plastic casing. There were several paintings visible, and a few pieces of furniture. I had spent little time there when I'd arrived, but the first place to start would be the paintings.

I got up and walked around the attic, trying to get a feel for their organization system. My footsteps echoed through the space as I walked. Luckily, whoever stored things up here seemed to have a method. There was an entire section dedicated to paintings, with dozens of canvases stacked together. I set the photos on a nearby table and tackled the first stack.

My mouth fell open as I went from painting to painting. There were several from local artists that had to be worth a lot of money. I recognized a few works from one of my favorites who'd died at the turn of the previous century and spent a few minutes admiring how he'd captured the light. I shook my head, forcing myself to get back to work.

By the time I'd gone through all five stacks of paintings, I'd pulled out the ones I needed for the entryway. I put those in a pile and went back to grab the photos I'd need to identify the various benches, coat tree, and other pieces of furniture that used to be in that room.

It took longer than I thought, but I'd located everything I could see in the photos and had everything moved to where I could easily access it. I was dripping in sweat, but thanks to how clean it was, at least I wasn't filthy. I had just started going through the dining room photos when I heard a strange buzzing sound.

I tracked the source to the intercom on the wall and hit the button, unsure of how the system worked.

"This is Brynn."

"Hello, dear. This is Mimi, the cook. I wanted to let you know lunch was ready. Shall I bring it up to you or would you like to come down here?"

I snapped up the chance to meet someone else who worked in this house, hoping I could interrogate her while I ate.

"I can come down there. Where are the kitchens located?"

"If you go to the east side of the attic, you'll find a large stairway that leads down to the servant's quarters. Once you go down the steps, turn to your left and you'll see a green door. That's the entrance to the kitchens. I'll be waiting for you."

"Thanks, be right there."

I released the button and looked around, trying to get a sense of my directions. Unfortunately, I wasn't blessed with the ability to navigate without a compass, a map, and a lot of luck. I shrugged and started walking, figuring I couldn't miss an enormous staircase, even in this big barn of a place.

Once I found it, I looked around for a landmark and spotted a statue. I could stack all the furniture I needed there, so it would be easier to get it downstairs. I trotted down the steps and followed Mimi's directions until I came to a green door that looked like it was covered in fabric. I snorted, feeling once again like I'd wandered into a British television show. Who in this day and age still used a green baize door to keep the servant's area separate? Then again, who actually still had servants?

I opened the door and followed a hallway that opened into a large, cheerful kitchen. I spotted a woman at the stove, and automatically smiled when she turned to me. Her hair was almost the same shade of red as mine, and I instantly felt a sisterhood with this woman. It was curly, too, but she had them piled on her head in a way that put mine to shame. Even though she had to be the same age as Reginald, she seemed younger somehow. Her wide mouth smiled back, and she wrinkled her freckled nose at me.

"You must be Brynn. I love your hair."

"Thanks, I love yours, too. I wish I could get my curls to organize themselves like you do."

"You're lovely. I've got your lunch tray over at the table. I'm just finishing up the preparations for Mr. Graff's meal," she said, pointing to a table over in the kitchen's corner.

She turned back to the stove as I walked to the table and slid a chair out. My mouth started watering as I looked at the feast she'd put on my tray. I was definitely had to save Bernie some of this somehow. She'd piled roast beef, mashed potatoes, and mixed vegetables on my plate, complete with gravy. I dug in and watched her work, marveling at her efficiency.

"Reginald mentioned you've worked here for some time. Do you enjoy working here?"

She paused as she plated up the food and looked over at me.

"It's a good place. I love cooking and it's nice to work with Reggie. We've been here so long it feels almost like we're one of the family. The Graffs have always been good to us."

I nodded as I forked up another piece of the tender beef and dipped it into the gravy. It was astonishingly good. I couldn't imagine eating like this every day, but I guess when you're wealthy, that's what you did.

"This is amazing, by the way. I've never had beef this tender."

She smiled again and nodded her head.

"Thank you. It's an old recipe from the previous cook. She'd

19

worked here after the gold rush. I'll be right back, dear, after I deliver this. If you need anything, the fridge is right over there."

I nodded as I went back in for mashed potatoes. I thought about Bernie and carefully secreted a few pieces of beef into my napkin and put it aside for him. By the time she returned, I'd cleaned my plate and was regretting it. I'd eaten too much, but I couldn't resist.

"Would you like any dessert, dear?" Mimi asked as she bustled back into the kitchen.

"Oh, no thank you. That was probably the best lunch of my life."

She dimpled and set to cleaning up the pots and pans. I stood and tucked the napkin with Bernie's treats into my back pocket, hoping my jeans wouldn't get stained. I brought my tray over and automatically started cleaning my dishes, to her obvious horror.

"You don't have to do that!"

"I know, but I was raised that whoever cooks doesn't have to clean. I don't mind."

We shared a companionable silence as I rinsed off my dishes and stacked them in the commercial dishwasher. This was an incredible house.

"Are you excited about the family reunion?" I asked as I dried off my hands.

Her mobile mouth quirked to the side, and she shot me a look that I couldn't quite interpret.

"It will be interesting, I'll say that. I've got to get to work making sure we have everything we'll need for the menu Mr. Graff approved."

I sensed she wanted to say more and leaned against the counter.

"Why will it be interesting?"

"The Graffs are a unique family with a lot of money. Let's just say a few of the younger members don't know the value of a dollar, and the older ones are worse. I honestly don't know what possessed Mr. Graff to invite them all here. God knows it won't be peaceful," she said, crossing herself.

"What do you mean?"

"Mr. Graff's children, Cynthia and Robert, have never gotten along. Their children are going in the same direction, even though they're all in their twenties. They act out by playing awful pranks on one another, and usually we endure the burden of cleaning it all up. It will be chaos, mark my words. I'd be surprised if someone doesn't end up dead."

"Dead? What pranks do these people play?"

Her face carefully arranged itself into a blank mask as she finished the dishes and started the gigantic machine.

"Forgive me, miss. I shouldn't have said anything. I'm grateful for this job and families are families. There are always a few members who don't get along with each other. It will be fine, I'm sure. I'll let you get back to work."

She'd cooled towards me so dramatically she seemed like an entirely different person. I nodded and headed back through the green door, wondering what she'd meant by her last comment. This place just kept getting stranger.

I put Bernie's treats out for him in the attic and didn't have to wait long for him to appear and wolf everything down. He blinked at me before rushing off again. I shrugged and got back to work, resigned to spending the rest of my day toiling away.

By the time I'd finished getting everything organized and laid out to be taken downstairs the next day, the light was fading and I had to turn the lights on to keep from falling over everything. The place still seemed cheery, but I could sense a deep disquiet that crept along my spine.

"Bernie? We need to get going."

"You don't need to yell," he said, from my feet.

I jumped in place and shook my head.

"How do you always do that?"

He shrugged his little kitty shoulders and started stalking towards the stairs.

"Let's get out of here. I'm shot and we need to figure out a plan for tomorrow. And I'm hungry again."

I gave him a mock salute behind his back before following him to the steps and picking my way carefully down. Despite my enormous lunch, I was hungry too. We didn't run into anyone as we wound our way to the entryway. I stopped at the giant door and looked around the dim space, trying to envision how it would all come together.

"Are you going to stand there all night?" Bernie asked, rubbing against my leg.

"Sorry, I got distracted. Why don't we pick up some pizza on our way home? I'll give Zane a call and see when his flight is supposed to land."

He followed me to my car and jumped in as soon as I opened the door. I got in and flipped on my lights before following the road down to the gates. Once again, they swung open automatically, and I drove off, mind spinning.

4

*F*our in the morning is an ungodly time of day to wake up, particularly when you stayed up too late talking on the phone the night before. I forced myself out of my comfy nest and shook Bernie awake before shuffling into the bathroom to get ready for the day. As I brushed my teeth, I grimaced at myself in the mirror.

I was never a morning person on the best day, and today? Well, let's just say I wasn't feeling this up before the birds thing. I reminded myself that I only needed to do this for one more day and this job would be done.

The smell of coffee wafted its way to my room, and I sniffed appreciatively, thanking my past self for having the foresight to use the timer on the machine the night before.

I looked into the mirror to finish tying up my hair and spotted Bernie behind me, where he was sitting on the floor, looking like a tiny, very disgruntled panther.

"Good morning," I said, faking a cheery tone.

His emerald eyes narrowed, and he stalked down the hall, ignoring me. A small part of me felt like doing a happy dance since I was finally the one waking him up, but I loved him too much to do that. I followed him to the kitchen and dished up a bowl of tuna to surprise him and hopefully put him in a better mood. A well-fed Bernie was a happy Bernie, and I needed both of us to be on our game today.

"There you go, buddy. Enjoy," I said, trying not to let the tuna fumes mess up my coffee vibes.

I poured myself a cup before filling my biggest travel mug with caffeinated goodness. I was hoping the steam would somehow fortify my brain, so I stuck my face over the cup and inhaled deeply. That was the stuff right there.

"You're awfully quiet this morning," I said, taking a sip.

Bernie picked his head up from his bowl and glared at me.

"And you're awfully cheery. I wonder if that's a coincidence."

He ducked his head back to his bowl as I gathered up my tote bag and tossed in my notebook and a few pens. I wasn't sure if I'd have time to stop by the library later in the day to research the Graffs and learn who the two ghosts might be, but I wanted to be prepared, just in case. I'd made good progress the day before, but there was still a lot to be done at the Graff place. My goal was to finish early, but I wanted to be realistic.

By the time I was ready, Bernie had already washed up and was sitting by his carrier, finishing his morning grooming routine.

"What time is Zane getting in? Hopefully, the big lug will help us today," he said, putting in one final swipe of his paw across his muzzle.

"He said he'd be landing around eight if the flight was on time. It will take him about an hour to drive up here from the airport, so I'm sure he'll be there to help when we need him. And what's this us business? Are you planning on lending a paw to move furniture around?"

"I could if I wanted to. Whether I want to remains to be seen."

He darted into his bag and turned around, nodding at me to hurry and zip the door closed. I was going to ask him how a small cat could move furniture, but I realized he probably could wiggle his nose or something and make everything move with minimum effort. Hey...

"Don't even think about asking me that question," Bernie said, growling under his breath.

I paused as I realized he'd read my mind, shrugging it off as yet another one of his fantastic talents that I didn't know about. Yet.

"Fine, but that would be really cool, Mr. Mind Reader. Well, no time like the present. Let's hit the road."

I turned up the music as I followed the highway into the canyon, hoping some music would power me through the drive. Luckily, there weren't any deer attempting to cross the road, and we made good time. The gate swung open, and I drove through, looking up at the house before parking under the overhang. It seemed somehow bigger than it had the day before.

"Could you let me out? There are a few things I want to look into before I join you in the attics."

"Sure thing, bud. Watch yourself. A few of the family members are due to arrive today, and from what Mimi said, they're not the nicest people."

"I'm pretty sure I can handle some entitled humans."

I unzipped his bag, and he rushed out, slipping past me like a shadow as I got out of my car. I paused at the door, unsure if I should ring the bell and risk waking everyone up. There weren't any visible lights on at the front of the house, so I followed the path around to the back, hoping to find the servant's entrance.

The kitchens were well lit, and I saw Mimi rushing around as I came up to the door and knocked. She glanced over her shoulder and motioned for me to come in.

"You're here early," she said, sliding a rack of cinnamon rolls out of the oven. "Good morning."

My stomach lurched and made a tortured noise. I slapped my hand over it, mortified.

"Good morning. Wow, those look amazing."

She grabbed a plate from the stack next to the stove and slid a cooled, iced roll onto it.

"Sounds like you could use some sustenance. Didn't Reggie answer the front door?"

I tore off a section of the roll and bit into it, closing my eyes as the flavors of vanilla and cinnamon competed for a gold medal on my tongue.

"I didn't want to wake Mr. Graff by ringing the bell, so I thought it would be best to come back here."

"Oh, sweetie, he's already gone for the day. But at least coming back here means you got to have a roll. You're too skinny."

I snorted and forced myself to eat the roll in small bites, rather than inhaling it like I wanted to.

"You're an incredible cook."

"Thank you," Mimi said, before icing the remaining rolls. "I'll have lunch ready by eleven-thirty. Take another roll. That's a long way off."

I followed her instructions eagerly and soon had it polished off too. Fortified with plenty of sugary goodness, I felt ready to attack my first task of the day, organizing the den.

"Do you mind if I go through the servant's quarters to get to the den? I'll be working there first, and then in the office."

"Absolutely. Whatever you need to do."

"Oh, I almost forgot. My boyfriend is coming to help me move some things. He should be here around nine."

"I'll let Reggie know. If you need anything, just ask."

I nodded and headed through the baize door, pausing as I tried to figure out where the front of the house would be. The wide stairs leading up to the attic were to my left, so I picked the right side and followed the long hallway.

Eventually, after a few twists and turns, I ended up in the house's entryway and looked around, trying to figure out where the den would be. I spotted the dining room and headed in that direction, since it was also on my list. I stopped as I took in the immense span of the table and tried to count the chairs before giving up at twenty.

"You'd think the Queen of England lived here," Bernie said from my feet.

I startled and looked down, noticing the smug expression he was wearing. He delighted in popping in unexpectedly.

"No kidding. Where did you go? You missed out on some cinnamon rolls that were out of this world."

He sniffed and rounded his eyes, pulling his starving cat routine.

"Oh, I guess you didn't save me any. That's okay."

I rolled my eyes as I knelt down to pet him.

"Sugar isn't good for cats, and you know that."

"I think we've established I'm more than your average cat."

"Okay, then. What are you exactly?"

He blinked and turned to look at the table again, ignoring my question.

"The den's over that way," he said, gesturing with his tail. "I think you should start in there."

I headed that way and glanced over my shoulder, noticing he hadn't followed.

"Aren't you coming, too?"

He shook his head and trotted off in a different direction, not bothering to answer.

I guess that told me. I kept walking and discovered a room off of the dining room that held several comfortable looking couches and chairs.

This would be where the family gathered to have drinks before dinner, I assumed, if my knowledge of high society television shows was correct. There was a large liquor cabinet in the corner, so I guessed I was at least mostly right. A few books were stacked on the tables, and I took a few minutes to browse through the titles, trying to get a feel for what Mr. Graff liked to read.

They were mostly about economics, from what I could gather from the titles, and seemed deadly dull. I kept going, making a mental map of what was in the room so I could compare it to the photos I had upstairs in the attic.

Satisfied I had a good idea of what was here, I headed back through the dining room to find the attic stairs.

The next few hours flew by as I kept working in the attic, locating

27

the artwork and a few pieces of furniture I'd need. Luckily, from the pictures, it appeared most of the chairs and couches were already in the room, which would save time. And my back.

I was searching through the art canvases again, hoping to find one more picture, when I heard footsteps approaching. I looked up, straight into Zane's blue eyes, and felt a bolt of pure joy stab itself through my heart.

"Zane! You're already here?"

He opened his arms, and I ran across the floor, resisting the urge to tackle him. Given he was well over six feet and heavily muscled, the odds of my tiny frame taking him down were small, anyway.

"It's so good to see you," he said, holding me close. "I missed you, but until I saw you over there, I didn't realize just how much."

He propped up my chin with a finger and gave me a quick kiss before crushing me into another hug.

"I missed you, too. I can't believe you're here. How was your flight?"

"We had a good tailwind, so I got to the airport earlier than I thought. I came right here. This is quite a place."

He released me from his bear hug, but kept one of my hands in his as he looked around the attic.

"It is enormous, isn't it? I can't imagine living in a place like this. I'd get lost at least ten times a day."

"I guess you'd get used to it after a while. I think this house is bigger than the apartment complex where I grew up in New York. So, what's the plan, boss?"

He turned his chiseled face in my direction and my stomach did its customary flip-flop again.

"Well, we need to move quite a few things downstairs. I've got everything ready to go. Once we've got it all arranged according to the photographs, we can move on to the next room."

"Wait, match the rooms to old photographs?"

I shrugged and led him to the back steps, where I had everything stacked.

"Essentially. Luckily, there aren't too many heavy pieces. I just need help with a few things if you have to get to work."

He stopped, dragging me to a halt, and smiled.

"Brynn, I haven't seen you in a week, and you've got an enormous job to finish. I'm here for you until it's done."

"You're the best. Did Reginald let you in?"

He laughed as we walked up to everything I had stacked at the top of the stairs.

"He did. That is probably the most awesome hair-do I've ever seen."

"Isn't it though? I thought your hair was luxurious, but I'm gonna have to give Reginald the edge," I said, winking at Zane.

"Hey, I'm wounded," he said, tucking a long strand behind his ear. "What's the deal with this job, anyway? You don't normally do stuff like this."

"Let's take a load downstairs and I'll tell you all about it," I said as I grabbed two paintings. "We'll get more done if we multitask."

By the time we'd made many trips up and down, I'd gotten Zane up to speed on everything and the entryway was done. I held up the photo and stepped back, wanting to make sure everything was perfect. Zane looked over my shoulder and nodded.

"Yep, this looks done. I still don't quite understand what they're going for with this project, but it sure looks nice."

"Let's head to the den so we can get the furniture arranged there before we bring down what we need for that room."

Zane followed me as I traced my way back through the dining room towards the den. He had the same reaction at the table that I did and was shaking his head as he joined me in the den.

"This place is like a museum."

"Isn't it though? Do you want to help me move this couch?"

He walked to one side as I grabbed my end of the couch and attempted to heave it. An icy breeze made the hair on my arms stand up and I paused, aware that we weren't alone anymore.

"Just what do you think you're doing?"

I turned to find the ghost of the older man I'd seen yesterday, standing behind me with that same sour expression on his face. Zane put his side of the couch down as he watched me.

"Brynn? What's going on?"

5

I refused to let the ghostly grump get to me. I turned towards him, noticing again his strong resemblance to Stephen, and pasted a sunny smile on my face. This would have been a perfect time for Bernie to show up, especially since he seemed to have a unique ability to help me communicate with recalcitrant ghosts, but I was apparently out of luck.

"And who do I have the pleasure of addressing?" I asked. "Or should it be whom? I could never get that straight."

"Whom. I am Cornelius Graff, and I demand to know what you're doing in this house."

"I thought you were a Graff! I've seen a few portraits and let me tell you, every one of you has the same expression. Do you come out of the womb like that, or is there a special class for the Graff heirs where you practice sucking on lemons?"

The ghost's eyes narrowed, but I kept smiling, feeling Zane's shoulder brush against mine as he joined me.

"Brynn, who are you talking to?"

"Zane, meet Cornelius Graff," I said, motioning towards the irate Cornelius. "I know you can't see him, but he looks like he ate a lime Jolly Rancher."

Zane bit his lip and nodded in the direction I'd pointed.

"Young lady, I don't know who taught you manners, but you've got some serious cheek coming into my house and treating me like this. I'll have you know in my day you would've been thrown out and given to your husband to beat."

Zane, thankfully, was used to listening to what appeared to be one-sided conversations with ghosts. He walked to the other side of the room to look at the paintings, knowing I'd fill him in as soon as the ghost was gone.

"Well, we're not married, but I don't think Zane would appreciate the suggestion."

"You've yet to answer my question. What are you doing here?"

"Stephen hired me to arrange the house as it was in what I assume was your time for an upcoming family reunion. I'd think you'd be happy about that. You were in the office when he hired me, so it's not like you're completely in the dark. Is he your son or grandson, by the way?"

Cornelius harrumphed and floated towards the liquor cabinet, gazing at it longingly before turning his sour expression back to me.

"A waste of time and money, if you ask me. Stephen is my grandson, and he shares his unfortunate profligacy with his father, Cornelius Jr. That boy went through money like it was water. I still don't know why he wants it done."

"I've asked the same thing," I said with a shrug. "How long have you been, well, um, in your present circumstances?"

He looked like he was around the same age Stephen was now, but I wanted to see how long he'd been haunting the halls of the manor, so to speak. And if he knew the female ghost Bernie had found.

"Time is irrelevant."

He dismissed my question with a wave that was eerily similar to Stephen's.

These people were definitely used to saying jump and having people rush to do their bidding.

"Is your son still around?"

"No, and may the saints be praised about that. I don't know where he is, and that is fine with me. I raised Stephen and although he inherited a few of his father's undesirable traits, he's most like me."

I wasn't sure if that was a good thing, but I needed to keep this surly ghost talking before he evaporated. I noticed the telltale wavering around the edges of his form that meant he'd spent almost all of his energy. He was looking at a bottle of scotch like a man who'd been trapped in the desert for forty years.

"Are you aware of a female ghost that is present here as well? Do you communicate with each other?"

His head turned towards me, scotch forgotten, and he narrowed his eyes even further.

"I do not know what you're talking about. Now, you've been thoroughly rude and I want you to leave. I've had enough of you."

I crossed my arms over my chest and raised my chin. I may not have wanted the job. I may not have had the foggiest clue why I was doing it. I may have wished I was back home snug in my bed rather than here. But I'd been hired to do the job, and I was going to do it.

"No can do. Besides, I'm supposed to have everything completed by tomorrow. If you don't want me hanging around, and you have nothing interesting to say, it would be in your best interests to let me get back to work."

Zane turned towards me with a raised eyebrow, surprised at my tone. Truth be told, I was surprised too. I had a soft spot for ghosts who were trapped on this side. I understood their circumstances and was driven to help them. This ghost, though? His thoroughly irritating attitude and high-handedness brought out the worst in me. I took a deep breath and willed myself to smile.

Cornelius surprised me by letting out a sharp laugh. I won't say he smiled, but he thawed slightly.

"I like your spirit. In my day we would have said you had gumption. Carry on," he said, with another elegant gesture, before stopping and looking at me with a serious expression. "Be careful. I don't know what Stephen has planned, but I have a bad feeling. Mark my words, blood will be spilled."

He slowly faded away, and I felt my heart rate spike at his words.

33

Zane must have sensed something and walked towards me, looking around the room.

"Is he gone?"

I tightened my ponytail before nodding and rolling my shoulders to release the rest of the tension I'd stored there during my conversation.

"Yes. He's a piece of work. Before he left, he said something odd."

"What did he say?"

I went back over to the couch we'd been moving before we were interrupted and smiled at Zane, determined not to dwell on the bad vibes I'd sensed from Cornelius.

"Let's get back to work and I'll tell you all about it."

We spent the next hour getting everything arranged in the den, while I told Zane about Cornelius and his attitude. Zane's face grew stony as I told him about Cornelius recommending I be beaten by my husband.

"It's a good thing I didn't hear him say that. You should've told him off."

"Actually, I felt like I was really rude. I don't know what came over me."

"Not rude enough. What do you think of his warning? Do you believe him?"

"Well, he's the second person to say something like that. Mimi, the cook, also has a bad feeling. I don't know."

"What do we do now?" Zane asked.

I checked the time on my phone and sighed. We still had another hour before lunch would be served. It wouldn't do me any good to dwell on the warning I'd received. With any luck, they would both be wrong.

"I guess let's go grab the paintings and decor items for this room. Maybe we can finish it before lunchtime."

Zane offered me his arm, and I felt a little like a princess as he led me through the dining room, even though I was wearing sneakers and jeans. As we worked, he told me about his trip to Vegas and what he'd learned at his security conference.

"It sounds like there's lots of new equipment out there," I said, trying to catch my breath after our latest trip down the stairs.

Yep, I definitely needed to spend some time in the gym. Although, I supposed this had to count as working out. At least a little.

"There were a few things I thought might be interesting in assisting you," Zane said, grinning and looking as fresh as a daisy as he came down the steps behind me.

"Really? Like what?"

"Well, it would be interesting to try out a few of the thermal imaging devices and maybe even a laser grid. I mean, I know you can see them, but sometimes it's hard to get ghosts to come out. It might help you detect where they are so you could focus on that spot. And it might help other people believe."

He'd come such a long way since we first met, when he'd disappeared abruptly after learning I could speak to ghosts. My heart warmed to see his interest in what I could do, and his desire to help. He knew about my upbringing in my small town, and how the kids had teased me mercilessly.

"It would be interesting to try them out, that's for sure. If one isn't too expensive, we might try it."

He beamed as he picked up the load I'd been carrying and added it to his own. His arm muscles bunched, temporarily distracting me as I followed him. What? I can't help it if he turns me into a silly teenager some times.

"I'll order one right away. I'd like to see if they really work, and since you can see the ghosts, we'll know for sure."

We finished getting the den organized and compared the pictures, just to make sure. I felt like collapsing on the couch, but the promise of another home cooked meal from Mimi propelled my feet towards the kitchen.

"Come on, Zane. I'll introduce you to Mimi."

I led him to the kitchen, and past the baize door, expecting to find Mimi hard at work. Instead, the place was empty, save for two covered trays that looked as though they belonged in a hotel. A folded note was left on the top of one, marked with my name. I glanced over at Zane before opening it.

Sorry I couldn't stay to meet your fellow. Please enjoy your lunches.

I showed it to Zane before uncovering the first tray. The smell of delicious fried chicken wafted out, and I swallowed hard, resisting the urge to drool. Zane's eyes popped open as he looked at my tray.

"This place is insane."

"Isn't it? It's like we're in a movie. Want to eat at the table over there?"

We took our trays to the table where I'd eaten the day before and silence fell as we demolished our lunches. If I'd thought the roast beef was delicious, it didn't hold a candle to the chicken. I remembered to put a little meat aside for Bernie, just in time to see him strolling into the kitchen, tail held high.

"I don't suppose you thought of me," he said, green eyes huge in his face.

"Of course I did, you silly goose. Come here, I've got plenty of chicken for you," I said.

"I saved him a piece, too."

Bernie bumped Zane's leg and let out a loud purr before tucking into his chicken noisily. I shook my head as I finished the rest of my lunch. Zane watched Bernie with a smile and picked the cat up as soon as he was done.

"Missed you, cat," Zane said, rubbing Bernie under the chin.

I smiled at the two of them, grateful for the way Zane was with Bernie. My cat had liked Zane from the first, something that had convinced me to give him a second chance when we'd fallen out. Seeing the two of them so close made my heart zip.

"Well, I'll do these dishes, and I guess we can get back to work."

"I'll help."

We got everything loaded into the industrial dishwasher and headed back up the steps to the attic, ready for our next task. Somehow, Zane still had plenty of energy, even after that enormous lunch. I was halfway up the steps when my phone rang. I smiled as I saw the name on my screen.

"Hey, Logan. What's up?"

"Are you running or something? Is someone chasing you? Are you in danger, Carrot Top?"

I rolled my eyes as I made it to the top of the steps. Okay, maybe I was breathing a little hard. But I wasn't about to admit to him.

"I'm not *that* out of breath. Just going up some stairs. And you know I despise that nickname."

"If you say so. Hey, is Zane back in town?"

"He is. He's helping me with a job, actually. Do you want to talk to him?"

"Nah. But since he's back, do you want to go out to dinner with Kelsie and me tonight?"

I looked at the pile of things we still needed to move and grimaced. Today was going to be a long day.

"I'll ask him. It's probably going to be a late dinner, though. I've got to get this done if not tonight, by tomorrow morning."

"What are you working on? That's fine. I don't mind a late dinner."

"It's a long story. I'll tell you tonight. Pick the place and let me know where we should meet you two."

"See you later, freckles."

"Bye."

I huffed out a laugh at my cousin's endless habit of using weird nicknames for me and ended the call, looking around for Zane. I spotted Bernie on the chaise again, watching Zane stack a few things into a crate.

"That's a good idea. I'm always terrified I'll drop something. Where did you find that crate?"

Zane looked up as I approached.

"I found a stack of them over there. What did Logan want?"

"He asked us to dinner. I accepted, if that's okay with you?"

"Sure thing. Where are we headed to next?"

"Next up is the dining room," I said, double checking through my notes. "There aren't any linens up here, but maybe they're stored down there. We'll have to check and see if we can find the exact table-cloth in the picture."

"The sooner we get this done, the faster we can be done for the day."

"I like the way you think," I said, heading off to find a crate. "Let's keep going strong. Once we're done with that room, we can finish with Mr. Graff's office."

6

*B*y the time we were done with the office, darkness was creeping over the hills outside and I was dragging my feet. It had been a long day, and if it hadn't been for Zane's help, I knew I'd still be slogging up and down the stairs.

I tweaked a few of the paintings before stepping back and holding up the original picture to check our work.

"That looks fantastic," Zane said, struggling to hide a yawn.

"Don't do that, you're contagious," I said, not even bothering to hide my camel yawn.

A loud gonging noise echoed through the space, startling both of us. I spotted Reginald, who'd been strangely absent for the entire day, trotting past the doorway. Zane leaned in close to whisper into my ear.

"Is this the Graffs?"

"I think it must be. And that's our cue to leave. Where on earth is that cat?"

I looked around for Bernie, but as usual, if I expected him to be in a place, he was nowhere to be found. A loud collection of voices came from the entryway and I figured Bernie would know we were leaving.

We seemed to be connected somehow, and all I could do was hope he'd show up in the car, or I'd have some awkward explaining to do.

Zane snagged my bag for me and we made our way to the entrance. A braying voice slowed my steps.

"Who's Godawful vehicles are parked right outside? Don't tell me daddy has lost all his money and has been reduced to driving those old things?"

My cheeks heated at the resulting laughter I heard as I realized they must mean my car. Zane's Jeep was a newer model, but mine was definitely edging towards old beater territory. I glanced at his face and noticed the skin on his neck was mottled red. I shrugged and kept walking, coming around the corner to spot several people with mountains of luggage crowded into the space.

"If you'll follow me, madam."

His face was completely devoid of expression, something I'd always aspired to, but never achieved.

"Who are these people?"

I stopped in my tracks as a tall, blond woman gestured in my direction. Her flawless skin looked like it was painfully stretched across her cheeks, and she was almost as emotionless as Reginald. This had to be Cynthia. I nodded and tried to put a friendly smile on my face.

"Hi, I'm Brynn Sullivan with Sullivan Staging, and this is Zane Matthews. Mr. Graff hired me. We'll get our vehicles out of your way."

She looked down her long nose as if I was some sort of strange bug who'd developed the ability to speak. The older man next to her rolled his eyes at her and gave me a lopsided smile before attempting to corral the two adult children who were engaged in a pushing fight, oblivious to the rest of us. Reginald stood by, apparently content to be treated like a potted plant.

"I see. Yes, remove them. I trust you're done with whatever father dearest has you doing?"

"The project will be complete in the morning."

She dismissed me with a glance and snapped at her children, who were still behaving like overgrown toddlers.

"Stephen! Stephanie! Stop that this instant. Reginald! Our rooms, please."

Cynthia's husband gave me an apologetic shrug before trailing after his wife. Her high-heeled shoes echoed like gunshots as she stalked away. Stephen and Stephanie passed without a glance at us, and I felt like a storm had lifted.

"Wow," Zane said, raising an eyebrow.

"You've got that right. Let's get out of here."

I walked outside and took a deep breath of cleansing, pine scented air. Mimi and Cornelius hadn't been kidding. If Cynthia's brother Robert was anything like her, I could see why their visit was dreaded.

"Where are we meeting Logan and Kelsie?"

"Shoot, I almost wish I hadn't agreed. Especially after that. Where on earth is that cat?"

"Don't let those people get to you. You know the type. Just ignore them and think about better things. Like what we're going to do after we eat."

His words perked me up immediately, and I felt a different flush work its way up my neck. I knew I probably looked like a tomato, but right now, I didn't care.

"Maybe we could skip dinner and go straight to that?"

My traitorous stomach took that moment to growl loudly, making Zane laugh.

"If there's anything I've learned, your tummy comes first."

"True. I'll text Logan before we leave if you want to follow me. I just hope Bernie shows up. I don't want to go back into that house."

"I'm right here, geez."

I stifled a screech as I realized Bernie was sitting right next to me, tail lashing back and forth. Zane chuckled and gave me a quick kiss before walking to his vehicle. My lips tingled as I watched him walk away.

"Are you always going to act like this around him?" Bernie asked, hopping in as I opened the door.

"Probably. Hey, where were you? Did you get to see the first half of the Graff family?"

"I was busy. And yes, I had the unfortunate pleasure of passing them in the hall on my way out here. I'm hungry. Text Logan and let's go."

"Yes, sir," I said, taking my phone out of my pocket. "Are you coming with us, or do you want me to drop you at home for some cat food?"

"What kind of question is that? And we better not have any quote unquote cat food in the place. We talked about that."

I texted Logan, and he answered that they'd be waiting for us at my favorite Mexican restaurant. The prospect of a bottomless basket of tortilla chips and a plate of tacos cheered me up immediately.

"Alright, bud. Let's go get our taco fix."

"Now we're talking."

I drove back into town, making sure Zane was behind me and didn't get lost on the twisting turns of the canyon. He pulled next to me in the parking lot and I sat for a second, remembering the first time we'd come here. Logan's date had let it slip that I talked to ghosts, and let's just say the dinner hadn't ended well. I smiled, feeling secure that we were in a much better place.

"I'll bring you in the bag and we'll get a table outside. It's still pretty nice out."

"Works for me. As long as I can have some queso, you won't hear any complaints from me."

I raised an eyebrow, knowing full well he was writing checks he couldn't cash, and Bernie let out a chirp. How could I stay mad at him when he acted like that?

Zane took the strap of Bernie's carrier and put it over his shoulder as we walked into the restaurant. I spotted Logan and Kelsie at the bar and waved them over to join us as we grabbed a table outside.

"Hi Brynn," Kelsie said as she picked a chair next to Logan. "How was your day?"

"Long. How about you?"

Kelsie was an old high school classmate who managed a historic hotel in Deadwood, where we'd found not only a grieving banshee but also a psychopathic hotel worker who'd been killing guests. Since then, she'd started dating Logan, and we'd been working on becoming friends, something I thought wouldn't have been possible when she was bullying me in school. Some people really can change.

"It flew by, so I can't complain."

"Hey big guy," Logan said, punching Zane softly in the stomach. "Thought you weren't coming back from Vegas."

Zane rolled his eyes at my cousin's antics, and Kelsie and I shared a look. Logan and I were close, and he'd been my staunchest protector through school. He was working on accepting Zane, and most of the time, he did a pretty good job of it.

"Nothing could keep me from coming back to Brynn," Zane said, leaning over and giving me another kiss.

He put Bernie's bag between our chairs so we could easily slip the cat tidbits throughout our meal.

"So, what are you working on, Logan?" I asked, reaching for a chip from the basket at the center of the table.

"A remodel project until the next house gets a foundation poured. How about you?"

I told Logan and Kelsie about my crazy new project, pausing as the server appeared to take our order. I didn't even have to think about ordering the taco platter with a side of queso, but everyone else took a little time going through the menu. Once she left, I fell back into my story.

"I know the family," Kelsie said, daintily dipping a chip in the hot salsa. "They've been around for generations."

I nodded as I tried the hot salsa and nearly lost my eyebrows as they shot up my forehead. Wow, that was a whole other level of hot. I drank some iced tea and briefly wished for milk until the heat finally subsided.

"That stuff should come with a warning. That makes sense, though, Kelsie. Stephen Graff said the house was built after the gold rush."

"And you're just organizing everything to match old pictures?" Logan asked. "That seems kinda weird."

"You're telling me. And it's going to be worth at least ten grand."

Logan choked on his salsa and coughed.

"What did you just say?"

"You heard me. Ten. I couldn't believe it either."

"Well, I know who's buying supper tonight," Logan said after he recovered from his coughing fit.

"Logan, that's not nice," Kelsie said. "It's your turn to pay."

"Hey, I'm not the one rolling in dough."

She rolled her eyes and turned to me, as Zane chuckled and dipped his chip. He was used to our dynamic and distracted Logan with an anecdote from the security conference.

"Did you meet any of the younger Graffs?" Kelsie asked. "I've heard they are, well, I guess you could say..."

"Entitled? Rude? Stuck-up? Stop me if you've heard this before," I said, laughing at her expression.

"Well, that's pretty much what I've heard. They've got a lot of pull, though. Stephen's kids, Cynthia and, oh, what was his name?"

"Robert?"

"Yeah. They're on many planning committees and historical boards. They have a lot of pull, even though they don't live here any more. I think they both moved across the state."

"Well, I should be done with the project tomorrow morning, so I won't have to deal with them for too much longer. How's Logan been feeling?"

I glanced over at my cousin as he laughed at something Zane was saying. Ever since he'd been poisoned, helping me with a case, I couldn't shake the feeling he'd nearly died because of me.

"He's fine and healthy as a horse. Brynn, don't keep kicking yourself. It wasn't your fault."

Kelsie squeezed my hand and gave me a reassuring smile as the server reappeared with our food. The smell of my tacos made my mouth water as the plates were passed around.

We spent the rest of the meal laughing, sharing stories, and enjoying the beautiful night. I passed Bernie a few pieces of meat and a quick lick of queso before he curled up in his bag to take a nap while we talked.

It was late by the time we finished our meal and went our separate ways. Zane followed me home and helped me get Bernie inside. The poor cat was tuckered out, making me wonder just what he'd been doing all day. As soon as he was out of his carrier, he went right back to my bedroom and curled on the bed. I checked on him before joining Zane in the kitchen.

"What a day. Thank you for all of your help. I couldn't have done it without you," I said, wrapping my arms around his toned middle.

"Anything for my girl. I missed you so much."

He raised my chin and leaned over, kissing me softly on the lips. My legs threatened to turn into jelly as the kiss deepened. He stepped back, chest heaving, and I couldn't seem to take my eyes off his lips.

"It's later than I thought. I'd better get home," Zane said, tearing his eyes away. "Do you need any help tomorrow?"

I swallowed hard, trying to make sense of the words he was saying before shaking it off.

"I'm sure you've got a lot to do, especially since you were with me all day. I should be fine. All that's left is just double checking everything and making sure Mr. Graff signs off on the project."

"If you need me, call," Zane said, stepping closer and giving me another kiss.

"You could stay," I said, breathless.

He rested his forehead on mine and I could feel his lips turn up in a smile as he groaned.

"I'd better not. You're exhausted, and need some sleep," he said, running his thumbs along my face. "I'll call you in the morning. Love you, Brynn."

"Love you, too."

He was right, even though I didn't want to admit it. My long day caught up with me and I felt like I could sleep standing up at this point. I walked him to the door, and he gave me another lingering kiss before stepping away and smiling wryly.

"Later, Sullivan."

"Later, Matthews."

I locked the door and went back to my bedroom to get into my pjs. Bernie didn't even move as I got under the covers and snuggled into the soft mattress.

7

*M*y alarm went off at five, prompting a severe case of déjà vu, as I laid in bed and wondered for the umpteenth time why I'd taken on this job. At least, thanks to Zane, I had little to do this morning. I rolled out of bed and noticed Bernie wasn't in his usual spot next to me. Weird.

By the time I got ready and went to the kitchen, he still hadn't made an appearance, and I was getting concerned. He wasn't one to miss a meal.

"Bernie?"

Nothing. The house was completely silent. I walked through each room, but my cat wasn't anywhere to be found. I walked back to the kitchen and fired up the coffeemaker, figuring he'd appear as soon as he figured out I broke the cats before coffee rule, but he was still mysteriously absent.

"I guess I'll just toss this can of tuna," I said.

"Why would you do that?"

"Gah! You've got to quit doing that, Bernie. Where have you been? I searched everywhere for you."

"I've been busy. You mentioned tuna?"

He wove around my legs and I sighed, unable to stay angry with the furry little beast. I cracked open the can and dished up his food while he waited impatiently on the counter. Whatever he'd been doing, he'd obviously worked up an appetite. I nearly spilled tuna on the top of his head when he stuck it into the bowl before I was done scooping.

"So, what were you doing that kept you so busy?" I asked, filling up my coffee mug and watching him closely.

"Can't talk. Eating."

I rolled my eyes and sipped my coffee, before opening up my notebook and going through the lists I'd made for this job. Everything had been checked off, but looking at the completed items made me feel better. Bernie finished his meal, scouring the dish spotless.

"Did you want to come with me this morning?"

He paused his washing up routine and looked at me. His green eyes looked tired, and I wished there was a way to stick a tiny camera on him so I could see where he went he pulled his disappearing act. The house was completely locked up, so I knew he couldn't have gone outside, but he seemed exhausted. Then again, he probably could go outside. He yawned, exposing his tiny pink gullet and sharp fangs.

"Not today. I need to do a few things."

"Like what?"

"Things. Shouldn't you be working?"

I gave him a smacking kiss on the top of the head, knowing full well that irritated him.

"I guess you've told me. Do you want anything while I'm out?"

"I could use some bacon. I don't mind chicken and fish, but variety is the spice of life."

"Bacon isn't good for cats."

He leveled his green stare at me and gave me his patented 'mom please' look.

"Do we really need to go over this again?"

"Fine. I'll grab some bacon. I shouldn't be gone long. Once I'm back, we can figure out what we're going to do next. Just because I got a nice paycheck doesn't mean we can rest on our laurels."

"I never do that."

I snorted as I loaded up my bag and filled up a travel mug. While the payment for this job was more than generous, I was looking forward to tomorrow when I wouldn't have to be up before the birds.

"See you later, Bernie."

He waved his tail in my direction as I walked out and locked up the door. Who would have thought a few weeks ago I'd be having conversations with my cat? I dearly wished I could understand what he was and what he did. As I started up my car, I debated going to look for Ned when I had more time. That wily ghost definitely knew more than he was saying, but I wasn't so sure I wanted to run into him again.

By the time I made it to the Graffs house, light was streaming over the canyon walls as the sun came up. It gave the valley bottom a beautiful glow, and I stopped for a second to take it in before heading up to the front door. I pressed the bell and waited for Reginald.

"Good morning, Brynn. It's good to see you," he said as soon as he swung open the massive doors. "I'm so sorry I wasn't available to help you with your project. I wasn't expecting to deal with the tasks Mr. Graff assigned me."

"No worries," I said. "I hope I'm not disturbing anyone by coming this early. I wanted to go through everything before my walkthrough with Mr. Graff."

"The bell doesn't sound in the guest wing where the family is, and Mr. Graff is already up. If you need breakfast, I'm sure Mimi has something for you."

"I'm okay, but thanks. Your wife is an amazing cook."

The older man grinned and his face lit up.

"She is, isn't she? Is there anything I can assist with since I fell down on the job yesterday?"

"I just need to make sure every item is accounted for and compare the pictures one more time. You can come with me if you'd like."

"I'm completely free at the moment. Where would you like to start?"

I dug through my bag for the pictures and sorted through them, figuring it made sense to start in the entry since we were already here. I handed him the photo and stepped back to take it all in.

"Do you see anything that's missing?" I asked.

Reginald looked back and forth, comparing the photos, and frowned.

"I see something missing, but I'm not sure how pertinent it is. See this painting? It's not there."

I leaned over his shoulder so I could see what he meant and paused. I remembered hanging it two days before, but the space where it had been was empty.

"Now that's odd. I know for sure I hung something there."

He shook his head and handed me the photo with a sigh.

"I'm sure it was, but one of those hellions probably moved it. They must have decided it would be fun to mess with you after meeting you yesterday."

I struggled to keep my temper under wraps as I realized he was probably right.

"Where would they have put it?"

"You know what? Let's go through each room and make a list. Then we won't be running back and forth. Something tells me this isn't the only thing they've done."

He took off at a fast pace towards the dining room and I trotted to keep up with him.

"Is this something that happens often?"

"Whenever the children are here, I'm afraid so. The delight in making mischief."

Children? They were definitely over eighteen and most likely older than twenty. I bit my tongue and pulled out my notebook as we stopped at the entrance to the dining room. Something felt off, but I couldn't quite place it.

Reginald was quiet as he studied the pictures.

"Aha. These three items have been moved around the room," he said, pointing out a vase and two statues. And the linens are backwards. I'll change that while you rearrange the items."

I moved around the room, collected the objects and put them

back where they were supposed to be, swearing softly under my breath, as Reginald got the table cloth fixed.

"Now for the den?" I asked, double checking the picture just to be sure I had everything right.

"Absolutely."

We found two pictures that didn't belong and one missing when we walked into the den. I felt an icy chill and looked around, expecting to see Cornelius, but he didn't materialize. Thankfully, the picture that didn't belong in the den went into the entryway, so I grabbed that and re-hung it before following Reginald into the office. He didn't knock, so I assumed Mr. Graff must be elsewhere in the vast house. I briefly wondered if Reginald had a tracking tag for his employer so he could easily find him.

"Let's see what we're working with in here," he said, frowning as he studied the photos.

We'd done a massive amount of work in here and my heart sank as I realized right away that the books had been targeted. A few volumes were placed the wrong way around, and the pranks didn't stop there. Whoever it was, Stephen or Stephanie, or possibly both, had spent a lot of time moving books into the wrong places. The paintings were all tilted, and of course, one was missing.

I heaved a sigh and got to work on the bookshelves, while Reginald focused on the paintings. By the time I was done, he'd completed his tasks, as the room was almost complete.

"We're just short one painting, huh?"

"It looks that way. I'm not sure where they would have hid the final one, though. We've been through all the rooms you were assigned."

"Probably back in the attic, or where they'd expect I wouldn't look. I'll run up there, if that's okay?"

"That's fine. I'll concentrate my efforts down here. If I find it, I'll buzz you on the intercom."

I went out into the hall and walked to the right, towards the rickety staircase that led to the attic. As I walked, I felt a chill that raised the hair on the back of my neck. I looked around but spotted nothing. The cold got more pronounced as I made it to the attic steps and I felt like someone was watching me. I glanced down the hall to make sure I was alone and whispered.

"Cornelius?"

The door to the steps slammed violently, and the cold grew worse. My arms broke out into gooseflesh as I felt a swirl of air go past me. This wasn't Cornelius, which meant it might be the ghost Bernie had spotted. I took a deep breath and tried again.

"Whoever you are, I mean you no harm. Is there anything I can do to help you?"

A soft, musical laugh filled the hall before cutting off abruptly. The air swirled near me again.

"Leave before you no longer can."

Well, that was certainly creepy. I squared my shoulders and reopened the door to the attic, scooting through it quickly just in case it slammed shut again. Bernie had been closemouthed about the ghost he'd found, and I wished I'd pushed him harder for more details. All he'd said was it was a woman dressed in clothing similar to the time Cornelius was from. I made it to the attic with nothing else happening and looked around.

Everything appeared as it had the day before, with nothing out of place. I walked around, looking behind pieces of furniture and against the walls before deciding the painting couldn't be up here. I was just about to give up hope when the intercom buzzed. I walked to the wall and pressed the button.

"Yes?"

"I've found it! It was behind the liquor cabinet of Mr. Graff's desk."

"Excellent. I'll be right down."

I hurried down the steps, but the air had warmed back up and I couldn't feel the ghost's presence any more. I retraced my steps back to Mr. Graff's office, where I found him and Reginald in conversation. My eyes tracked to the wall where the painting should be and I relaxed when I saw Reginald had already replaced it.

"Ah, Miss Murphy. Reginald was telling me my precocious grandchildren played a little prank on you. I trust everything has been set to rights?"

I forced a smile I didn't feel and tried to not think ill thoughts towards the Graff grandchildren. If I'd done such a thing, I wouldn't have been able to sit for a week, even though I was older than they were.

"Yes, everything is where you specified it should be. Would you like to do a walkthrough with me?"

He waved his hand in that familiar elegant gesture and shook his head.

"No, it all seems in order."

"Great. Would you like me to invoice you, then?"

"Actually, I have one more request before I can remit your payment."

My heart sank as I realized I wasn't quite done with this strange job and even stranger people just yet.

"Yes?" I asked, dreading his answer.

"I'd like you to attend the family meal tonight. You can, of course, bring a guest. The dress code is formal and you'll need to be here at six sharp."

"Oh, I don't want to intrude. I can just invoice you and you can mail me a check when you get it."

"I insist," he said, steel in his tone.

"But..."

"Six sharp. If you do not attend, you will not receive your payment. That is all."

He waved at Reginald to escort me out, and I did my best to reel my jaw back up to its proper place. I had to go to a dinner with these awful people or not get paid?

Reginald nodded his magnificent pompadour towards the door, and I followed him out, completely stunned. Once we were at the door, he opened it and nodded at me.

"Well, I guess I will get to see you again. You'll have to excuse Mr. Graff. He is quite particular."

"I don't even know what to wear. What does formal mean, exactly?"

Reginald slowed his steps and gave me a gentle smile.

"A nice dress for you, and a suit and tie for your gentleman friend will be perfectly suitable."

I nodded, overwhelmed, before walking outside. I'd never heard of such a thing before. After I got back in my car, I called Zane. I could hear the smile in his voice when he answered.

"Good morning, love."

"I'm not so sure it's good," I said, still trying to make sense of that conversation with Stephen.

"Uh oh, that doesn't sound good. What's up?"

I put the phone on speaker as I started up my car and drove down the driveway, searching for the right words. By the time I finished telling Zane about my morning, he was laughing.

"If you think it's funny, I'm telling it wrong."

"Oh, it will be fun. We'll get some free food out of the deal and a chance to see how the other half lives. I'll run home after work, grab a suit, and meet you at your house at five."

"You've met them and you can still say that?"

He laughed again, and I could picture him shaking his head.

"It will be fine. Besides, you need to get paid for all that work. We'll eat some rich people's food, collect your check and go home. What could go wrong?"

"Oh, now you've totally jinxed us," I said, wailing. "We can't go now. The money doesn't matter. I don't want to be around those people any more than I have to. I'll just chalk it up to an interesting few days and call it good."

"Brynn, seriously, it will be fine. I'll see you at five. Do you have a dress?"

I thought about my wardrobe and grimaced. The vast majority of my closet was full of tee shirts, jeans, and hoodies. My work meant I regularly got dirty and ripped things, and dressy clothes weren't really my style.

"I might have something. I guess I know what I'm doing for the rest of the day," I said. "This had better be worth it."

"I can't wait to see you."

"I bet you look handsome in a suit," I said, warming up to the idea.

"I'll let you be the judge of that. See you at five."

I ended the call and thought of Zane all dressed up as I drove back into town to run some errands. He looked incredible in polo shirts and slacks, so I could only imagine what he'd look like in formal wear. My mood improved as I found the bright side. Maybe dressing up and sitting through a dinner wouldn't be so bad after all. I remembered I needed to grab some bacon and headed to the grocery store first.

8

*a*s I walked up the steps to my house a few hours later, I saw Bernie's sleek black head pop up in the window and my heart warmed. It had been forever since he'd done that simple gesture and it made my day. He came jogging over to me as I opened the door and I scooped him up for cuddles.

"I missed you, bud. Are you okay?"

He buried his head under my chin and purred loudly before straightening and squirming to be let down.

"I'm fine," he said, licking his flank. "What's going on? Your vibe is different."

"Well, I've been *invited* to dinner at the Graffs. And if I didn't accept the invitation, I wouldn't get paid. So, Zane is coming with me and he's picking me up at five. I've got nothing to wear and no idea how one even comports oneself at a meal like that."

He stopped grooming and fixed his green eyes on me, his expression sharp.

"Really? Hmm. That's interesting."

"Why is that interesting? And I think the adjectives you're looking for are terrifying, maddening, and strange, not interesting."

"No reason."

I glanced at him as he attempted to look innocent, something I rarely fell for. Okay, maybe I fell for it. A lot. He was pretty irresistible.

"What aren't you saying?"

"Why would you think something like that?" he asked, eyes rounding. "I'm hungry."

"Fine, I'll get you something to eat and then I need to go through my closet. I don't think I have anything appropriate, but I really don't want to go shopping for a dress I'll wear once."

"More dishing of food, less whining."

I rolled my eyes as I followed Bernie into the kitchen and complied with his demands. I opened the fridge to see if I could slap something together for lunch, but my stomach twisted at the thought of food. I closed it and headed back to my bedroom to sort through my pitiful collection of nice clothes.

I unearthed a pair of dusty heels in the back of my closet and eyed them suspiciously. There had to be a reason they'd been relegated to the dark recesses of my closet and forgotten. They were probably horribly uncomfortable. However, they were black, and I'd hoped they'd clean up with a little soap and water. That solved, I started going through the rack, pulling out the few dresses I actually owned.

I was holding up a printed floral and trying to decide if it would work when Bernie strolled into the room and hopped on the bed.

"No."

"But it's pretty."

"No," he said, settling down in a loaf position. "What else do you have?"

I grabbed a black dress and held it in front of me before facing him.

"What about this one?"

"It makes you look pale. Well, more pale than usual."

I grumbled under my breath as I went back through my closet, hoping something appropriate would magically appear, before finding a green dress I'd forgotten I even owned.

"I think this is it," I said, holding it up for Bernie's inspection.

"That's the one. Don't forget to clean those heels. I think there's a dust bunny in one that's bigger than I am."

I grabbed a washcloth from the bathroom and scrubbed at the shoes, relieved to see they looked better when I was done. As I got dressed, I eyed Bernie, wondering what he'd been up to that morning.

"So, you were going to tell me what you were doing this morning before I left..."

He looked at me before gently nipping at one of his claws.

"I don't recall saying anything about that."

I met his eyes in the mirror as I pulled the dress on over my head and he looked away, refusing to make eye contact. I shrugged as I smoothed the fabric over my hips. Let him keep his secrets. I played with my hair, trying it up and down before deciding to wear it down.

"Oh, I think I had a run-in with the other ghost you met," I said, remembering my encounter in the hallway.

He stopped picking at his nail and slowly looked at me, concern clear on his face.

"You did what now?"

"I did nothing. I simply needed to go into the attic and before I could go up the steps, I felt a chill and a door slammed."

He sat up straight on the bed, fur fluffed.

"You need to be careful of her. She's not what she seems."

"That seems to be a running theme around here. Speaking of things that aren't as they seem..."

"Never mind that. Did she say anything to you?"

"Yes. She said I should leave before I no longer could or something like that. She laughed before she said it."

"That settles it. I'm coming with you."

"Why? I'd think a human dinner party would be the ultimate bore for a cat."

"You might be surprised. What time is it?"

"A little before five. Why?"

"Shouldn't you finish getting ready? Zane's almost here."

He thumped down from the bed and jogged into the living room,

59

leaving me standing there with way more questions than answers. Again. I shook my head and finished getting ready. For once, my curly hair cooperated, and I liked the way the green dress looked with my red mop. I joined Bernie as I heard Zane's Jeep pull up outside.

I opened the door before he could knock and smiled at him, drinking in the sight of him in a suit. His broad shoulders looked even wider, and he seemed somehow taller.

"Wow, Brynn. You look amazing," he said, grinning. "You're always beautiful, but wow. I can't take my eyes off you."

He leaned close for a kiss, and I couldn't help but inhale the scent of his shaving lotion. He almost smelled better than he looked, and that was saying something.

"Yeah, yeah," Bernie said, trotting past and sitting at the Jeep's door. "Let's get a move on."

Zane looked over his shoulder at the cat before turning back to me.

"I take it he's coming with us?"

I nodded as I reached down to snag Bernie's carrier. He might not like riding in it, but it made me feel better.

"He insisted."

Zane tucked his dark hair behind an ear before offering me his arm with another grin.

"Your carriage awaits, my lady."

I flushed a little as he led me to the passenger side, where Bernie was impatiently waiting. I put the bag down so he could jump in and got him zipped up before Zane put him in the back seat. As we drove off, Zane entertained me with stories about a new client who was exceedingly particular. The trip flew, and we were pulled up in front of the Graff's house before I knew it. I swallowed hard as Zane walked around to my side. What was this dinner going to be like?

I quickly unzipped Bernie from his bag, and he rushed past me as Zane opened the door. I stumbled a little as I got out and Zane put his muscular arm around my waist to steady me. He looked down at me and searched my face, his eyes worried.

"Everything okay?"

"Yeah, just nervous."

"It will be fine. Just be yourself. If they don't like you for who you are, they don't deserve your time."

I felt like Cinderella as he led me to the massive front door. He rang the bell and Reginald appeared, smiling brightly as his white hair shone in the entrance's light.

"Don't you two look like a picture? Please, follow me."

He led us to the den and announced us as we stood in the doorway. My face felt hot as everyone in the room turned to look at me. Cynthia looked down her long nose at me and sniffed.

"Why are they present?"

Reginald ignored her and gave me a reassuring smile before walking out of the room. I didn't blame him, and fervently wished I could follow. Zane put his arm back around my waist and I felt steadied by his contact. I slapped a weak smile on my face as I looked at the unfriendly faces. A tall man, who could have been a double for Cornelius Graff, walked towards us and stuck his hand out.

"I'm Robert. Welcome to our little gathering. I see you've met Cindy already. And most likely her heathens. My pair is right over there, Robert Jr. and Sophia," he said, nodding towards a couch, where two younger adults were engrossed in their phones, not even registering our presence. "My wife, Lucinda, is over there."

"It's nice to meet you," Zane said, shaking his hand. "Is anyone else coming?"

I took the opportunity while they were talking to look around the room. Everything was where it should be, and I breathed a sigh of relief.

"I hope you're not too mad at our little trick," said a voice by my ear, making me jump.

I turned to face Stephen, wishing for a split second I could slap his little grin off his face. Stephanie was with him, and was giggling in a high pitched tone that made the hair on the back of my neck stand up.

"Not at all," I said, forcing another smile. "It comes with the territory."

Stephanie's giggles trailed off, and she cocked her head to the side, looking at me curiously.

"You're not mad?"

"Why would I be? I look at it as an opportunity to test my skills."

Zane turned towards me and nodded at the two, before looking at the where Robert Jr. and Sophia were still tapping away on their phones.

"Do you plan to stay in the area long?" he asked.

Robert looked up at Zane and shrugged.

"Probably not. There's not much to do here until the snow flies. Even then, these hills the locals call mountains don't hold a candle to Breck."

I avoided rolling my eyes, but it was a near thing. I felt a slight chill on my exposed arms and looked around the room, wondering which ghost was about to make an appearance. I didn't have to wait long until Cornelius popped into sight, wearing his familiar sour expression.

He looked around the room and stuck out his chin before shaking his head. We briefly made eye contact, and he gave a ghostly harrumph before drifting towards the liquor cabinet, where Cynthia and her husband were standing.

"What are you looking at?" Stephen asked, as Stephanie giggled next to him.

"Oh, um, that painting over there. I think it's crooked," I said, before walking over to the wall and nudging the painting a little.

I needed to be more careful. Luckily, Zane distracted the two, and I followed Cornelius, wishing I could talk to him openly.

He was standing against the wall, staring at the scotch bottle again, before meeting my eyes. He nodded once and went back to staring.

"I can't imagine why father felt it necessary to include the help in our gathering," Cynthia said loudly, elbowing her husband.

He coughed into his fist and shot me an apologetic look before murmuring something to his wife I couldn't hear. As he walked out of the room, I realized I'd never been introduced, and didn't even know his name.

Not wanting to engage Cynthia in conversation, I quickly grabbed a set of glasses and splashed a little club soda into each, forgoing the alcohol. Something told me I'd need to keep a clear head tonight.

Zane's arm brushed mine as he came up next to me, smiling at Cynthia. She sniffed again and sailed off toward her niece and nephew, leaving us blessedly alone.

"Can we go home yet?" I asked out of the corner of my mouth before handing him his drink.

He took a sip and raised an eyebrow at me before answering.

"It will get better. Where is Stephen Graff?"

I looked around the room again, noticing that the younger Stephen had left the room.

"I'm not sure. How long do you think the old drinks before dinner ritual will last?"

"Who knows?" he asked, tilting his glass and draining it. "But I have a feeling I'm going to need more than club soda to get through the night. I'm still reeling from Stephen and Stephanie. Do you think Cynthia could have been any more obvious in her attempts to curry favor with her father?"

I snorted loudly and covered it up with a cough before glancing over at Cornelius, who'd transferred his attention to the door. The elder Stephen was standing there, observing his family. I turned to take it in, noticing his son, Robert, was no longer in the room.

Cynthia rushed to her father, smiling as widely as her fillers would allow.

"Daddy, it's so good to see you," she said, leaning her head on his shoulder.

He shrugged, bumping her head, and moved away.

"Where is everyone? And why are Robert Jr. and Sophia still on those dang devices? I told you there would be no devices allowed at the table," he said, his voice cracking like a whip.

I swallowed hard and glanced at Zane. He'd pulled himself up to his full height, and I wished I could hide behind him as Stephen Graff's eyes turned towards me. He surprised me by smiling widely.

"There you are. You must be Brynn's date. I appreciate you attending. After all, I wanted you to experience for yourself the fruits of all your labors. Particularly since you had to do some tasks twice," he said, leveling an angry look at Stephanie.

She blanched and looked at her mother, who was standing in the doorway twisting her hands together. Reginald appeared in the doorway, clearing his throat, and Cynthia jumped before taking something from his hands. The butler turned on his heel and left.

"Daddy, Reggie brought your favorite drink," she said, rushing to Stephen's side.

He grimaced at her before a loud noise from the window pulled everyone's attention.

"Ouch!"

"Stephanie, darling, what's wrong?" Cynthia asked, almost furrowing her brow.

"Nothing, mommy. I stubbed my toe."

Stephen took the drink from Cynthia's hand and turned back towards us.

"I'm surrounded by horrible disappointments," he said, taking a large gulp of his drink. "Except for you. I've got your payment in my office. Once this farce is over, you may take your payment."

I blushed as I felt the eyes of the surrounding Graffs narrow in my direction. Zane put his hand on my back and I took a deep breath and tried to smile.

Cornelius snorted behind me, and I resisted the urge to peek over my shoulder. Stephen's face was flushed, and he sat the tumbler he was holding down on the liquor counter. He took a handkerchief out of his pocket and dabbed at his forehead. I looked at him, concerned, as his face twisted in what looked like pain.

He gulped a breath and turned towards me to say something before grabbing at his throat.

"I…"

He crumpled to the floor at my feet, and the room erupted into chaos as I knelt next to him, grabbing his hand.

"Mr. Graff, what's wrong?"

He looked like he was trying to say something, but his face went rigid and nothing came out besides an awful gurgle. Zane joined me and gently shook him.

"Mr. Graff?"

Zane's eyes met mine, and he shook his head sharply as he reached for Stephen's neck to feel for a pulse. I could tell from the way his eyes shut he didn't find one. He handed me his phone, and I immediately dialed 9-1-1.

"I told you something would happen," Cornelius said before vaporizing behind me as I talked to the dispatcher.

Zane set to work trying to resuscitate Stephen as Cynthia shouted and dove for her father, pushing Zane away.

"You'll hurt him, you big monster. Leave my daddy alone," she said, wailing as she pounded on her father's chest.

Zane kept working, and I tried to steer Cynthia away so she wouldn't stop him.

"You! You did this," she said, tearing away from me and pointing her finger in my face. "You killed my daddy."

9

$\mathcal{M}$y mind was several steps behind, still trying to make sense of what happened and why Cynthia would accuse me. She was noisily wailing on the shoulder of Lucinda, who was glaring daggers at me. Stephanie was carrying on like an air-raid siren in the background, while Robert Jr. and Sophie were talking on the couch, their blond heads together. I shook my head and made eye contact with Cynthia.

"I don't know why you would think I would kill your father, but I assure you, I'm not the one who did this," I said, trying to keep my voice from shaking.

Reginald hurried into the room, a look of abject horror on his face as he saw his employer lying on the floor. He seemed lost as he looked around the room.

"What is going on here?" he asked, zeroing in on me.

"Mr. Graff took a drink of whatever you brought him and fell over dead a short time later," Zane said before placing his coat over the face of Stephen Graff and standing next to me.

"No, it can't be. It just can't be. Mr. Graff always had the same drink before dinner. Vermouth with an olive. I brought it from the kitchen since it needs to be chilled. I don't understand."

I glanced at the glass on the liquor cabinet, realizing we needed to preserve any evidence that might remain. I nudged Zane with an elbow and motioned towards the cabinet, hoping he'd understand what I meant.

Zane nodded and positioned himself in front of it before looking back at Reginald.

"I'm going to need to make sure no one leaves this place. Brynn already called the police. Several people left the room before this happened and we need to account for everyone."

"Right away, sir," Reginald said, hurrying out of the room.

Cynthia abruptly quit crying and narrowed her eyes at Zane.

"Well, when they get here, you can have them arrest your girl-friend. It's obvious she's the one who did this. I can't believe my daddy is dead."

Zane squared his shoulders and leveled a glare at her.

"Stop saying that. Brynn wouldn't hurt a fly. She also is probably the only other person in this room, besides me, who didn't have a motive to kill your father."

Robert and Cynthia's husband walked into the room, talking together in hushed tones. They stopped when they saw the body on the floor and looked around the room. Cynthia ran to her husband and threw her arms around his neck, and began sobbing loudly again. This woman had an ability to switch moods like no one I'd ever met before, and I glanced at Zane to see his expression. It mirrored mine, a combination of shock, disgust, and sadness. Stephanie joined them and added her loud wails to the chorus.

Robert walked over, wearing a strange expression, and picked Zane's coat off of his father's face before shaking his head.

"Too bad, old man. We left too much unsaid."

He dropped the coat and walked past us to pour himself a drink. Reginald came back in, his pompadour askew, and walked over to us, drawing my attention away from the Graffs.

"I've accounted for everyone except Stephen, the younger. There's a vehicle missing as well," he said, leaning close to us so he wouldn't be overheard. "I believe he has flown the coop."

"Are there security cameras?" Zane asked.

Reginald nodded.

"They're not manned, but we have a system set up. The security room is locked, and I have the key on me at all times," Reginald said, patting his vest pocket. "I will, of course, make sure the police have access to the security feed."

The bell sounded for the door, and Reginald quickly smoothed his hair before giving us a brisk nod and heading out of the room. I wrapped my hand around Zane's arm.

"What do you think is going on?" I asked.

Zane shook his head, his light blue eyes filled with confusion.

"We've got way too many suspects. Stephen, the younger's disappearance doesn't look good."

"Gosh, I feel like we're trapped in some crazy English murder mystery with these names. Stephen the younger. For crying out loud. Why do you think Cynthia's first reaction was to blame me?"

He tucked his hair behind his ear and shrugged.

"She might want to turn the spotlight on you to get it off of her. She's the one who handed him the drink."

A familiar voice echoed through the room, and I turned my head to see Dave Beldon, the sheriff of our little community, standing in the doorway to the den.

"Everyone, I need quiet. Where's Brynn?"

I popped my head around Zane's frame and waved to Dave.

"I'm over here, Sheriff."

"Wait. You know her?" Cynthia asked, her face mottled red as she looked between us.

"Yes, ma'am," Dave said, nodding for me to join him. "I've known her since she was a little girl."

"Well, it's obvious we won't get justice in this case. A local-yokel sheriff who's friends with the woman who killed my daddy. I want the state police called in. Immediately."

Dave's jaw tensed, and he glanced at the body on the floor before turning his attention back to Cynthia.

"I'll take it under advisement. Until then, I need everyone to move out of this room and into the dining room so I can take your statements. The coroner is on his way here and we need everyone out."

Grumbles filled the room as the Graffs filed out. I noticed that beyond a few glances at the body, no one other than Cynthia and her daughter appeared to be that upset. Robert Jr. and Sophia followed, while never taking their eyes off their phones. Dave hooked his thumbs through his duty belt and looked between us.

"So, what happened here? And why is a woman of that age still calling him daddy?"

I fought an urge to giggle and took a deep breath before recounting everything I'd seen. Zane broke in a few times with his own observations, but by the time the coroner arrived, we'd given Dave a complete run-down. We stepped to the side while the coroner worked and I continued the thread.

"Reginald brought Mr. Graff a drink, Cynthia took it from him to give to her father. Once he had a drink, it was only a short while before he was clutching his throat and he was gone. Zane made sure no one touched the glass after it happened. It's right here on the cabinet."

"Do you suspect poison?" Dave asked, looking at Zane keenly.

A few weeks ago, Dave had hired Zane as a special consultant. It was obvious he respected Zane's opinion, and Zane's background in the military.

"I do," Zane said, nodding. "While I was attempting to resuscitate him, I noticed a strange taste on his lips. I don't know the type of poison, but I'm almost one hundred percent sure that's what killed him. You should be able to have your lab analyze the contents of the glass."

Dave sighed and removed his cowboy hat to scratch his head.

"We'll secure this room and make sure no one else can enter. My deputies should be here in a few minutes. What are you two doing here, anyway? I wouldn't have thought these people were your usual crowd."

"You're telling me. Mr. Graff hired me to stage a few rooms before this family reunion. I had to match the decor to old pictures he had of the place. He never said why he wanted it done, just that it had to be completed before everyone showed up. Once I was done, he said if I wanted to get paid, I needed to attend tonight's dinner."

Dave raised an eyebrow and looked at me.

"Don't you think that's a little odd? I mean, I guess rich people have their whims, but matching rooms to pictures?"

"I thought the same thing, but now I'm not so sure," I said, looking up as Reginald entered the room.

"Sheriff, I've made sure everyone, including Mimi, is in the dining room. All the family is accounted for, minus Stephen the younger, of course. I can provide you with the details of the missing vehicle if that will be of help."

"That would be helpful. Thanks," Dave said.

Reginald left the room and Dave leaned in closer to us.

"What are the odds the butler did it? You said he was the one who brought Mr. Graff the drink."

I looked at him, horrified.

"I don't think Reginald did it, Dave. He was truly upset when he saw Mr. Graff on the floor. He wasn't acting, I'm sure of it."

"He's still a suspect, Brynn. Who else works here?"

"His wife, Mimi, is the cook. He mentioned a few workers who come in occasionally, but they're the only ones who live here."

"Are you, um, picking up on anything?" Dave asked quietly.

"There are two ghosts, for sure. I haven't seen the ghost of Mr. Graff if you're asking, but it's entirely possible he might appear. It can take a little while sometimes."

He heaved another sigh and adjusted his duty belt on his narrow waist.

"All right, then. If you see anything, let me know. It would be helpful if his ghost would appear and point the finger, so to speak. Where would you recommend I set up to interview everyone?"

"Mr. Graff's office would be the best spot. It's removed enough for the dining room so you can have privacy with each family member. I'll show you where it is."

Dave stopped to chat with the coroner and I scanned the room, hoping to see Mr. Graff's ghost. While I wouldn't wish getting trapped between planes on anyone, Dave was right. It would be helpful if he had. As I walked out of the room, I suddenly thought of Bernie. Where on earth was he? With everything that happened, I'd completely forgotten he'd insisted on coming with us. Did he know something was going to happen?

Two deputies walked into the room, and we stood outside the door as Dave gave them directions on what he wanted them to do to secure the room.

Once he was done, I motioned for him to follow us and we walked into the dining room. Cynthia's voice rang out, silencing everyone as she stood from her seat at the table.

"I demand to know what is going on here."

Dave tipped his hat in her direction and gave her a friendly smile.

"What's going on is that we have a dead man, and any of you could have been the one to kill him. I need to interview every single person who was present, including your son, ma'am. Do you have any idea where he went?"

Cynthia's face blanched, and she sat down, hard.

"I'm sure he's around somewhere," she said, in a much smaller voice.

"Well, we need to find him. I suggest you get in touch with him and make sure he delivers himself. That, or I can put out an A.P.B. on him. It's up to you."

She nodded and gripped her hands tightly together.

"He says he's on his way back," Sophia said, finally tearing her eyes away from her phone. "I've been texting him for the past fifteen minutes."

Dave nodded his head.

"Alright. I'm going to get set up and then I'll call the first witness. In the meantime, no one should leave."

He tipped his hat again and followed us as I led the way to Mr. Graff's office. I struggled with the massive French doors and Zane helped me get them open. The room was dark, and it took me a few seconds to find the switch.

Dave let out a low whistle as he took in the book collection that lined the shelves.

"This is quite an office," he said, walking around to the desk.

I felt a familiar tail wrap itself around my ankle and looked down to see Bernie sitting there, eyes narrowed. I almost slipped and talked to him before closing my mouth abruptly.

Dave turned around and did a double take as he realized my cat was in the room.

"Is that... you know what? Never mind. I've given up being surprised where you're concerned."

Bernie nodded and blinked at Dave, causing the older man to chuckle and shake his head.

"Sorry, Dave. He came with us, but I lost track of him until now. He likes to come to my job sites with me," I said.

He waved me off and walked over to the desk, looking at the top of it, before slowly spinning to face me.

"Brynn? What do you make of this envelope?" he asked, holding it out to me.

I took it from him and felt my stomach lurch as I read the writing. Zane leaned over so he could see it. His eyebrows hiked up as he read it aloud.

"In the event of my death, this letter is to be opened by Brynn Sullivan," Zane said, looking at me. "What on earth?"

10

When I opened the envelope, I found a hand-written note, and a check fluttered to the floor. Zane bent to pick it up while I started reading. By the time I got through the first sentence, I shakily sank into a chair and shook my head. This couldn't be happening.

"Brynn, are you okay?"

"Yeah, I just can't believe this," I said, re-reading the opening to the letter. "It says here, 'If you're reading this, I've been murdered, just as I expected I would be. You should know I hired you under false pretenses. Bob told me of your special abilities and your past successes at solving murders. Now, I need you to solve mine. All I know is someone in my family was plotting to kill me. I've taken precautions, but in the event they fail, I will need your help. You will, of course, be compensated for your efforts. In the drawer of my desk, you'll find an updated will that I had drawn up yesterday. Reginald served as one of my witnesses. You can trust him implicitly. Below my will, you will find a dossier containing information about all of my relatives. I trust it will be useful.' I simply cannot believe this."

"I don't think you'll believe this either," Zane said, handing me the check.

I read the amount, and re-read it, my mind refusing to comprehend the amount.

"This is a check for fifty thousand dollars," I said, handing it across to Dave. "I don't understand any of this."

Dave pulled a pair of reading glasses out of his shirt pocket and scanned the check before motioning for me to pass him the letter. Zane took the chair next to mine and took my hand in his as Bernie jumped into my lap and leaned against my chest.

"You had no sign he had an ulterior motive?" Dave asked, looking at me over his glasses.

"No. Why would he do something like this? What did he mean he'd taken precautionary measures?"

"I think we're going to ask your butler friend about that. You know how I feel about having civvies messing around with my cases, Brynn. And you usually ignore that and help, anyway. But this time, the victim specifically requested your involvement."

His eyes twinkled as he took off his cowboy hat and leaned back in Stephen Graff's chair.

"I think you're right. If you want to go through the will and the dossier, I'll go grab Reginald," Zane said.

I leaned closer, cradling Bernie close to my chest as Dave rummaged through the desk drawer.

"Here it is," he said, slapping the will down on the table. "Let's have a peek, shall we?"

He read through the first page before propping his glasses on the top of his head and pushing it towards me while he went to the second page. I scanned what he'd given me, and stopped to re-read it, mouth open.

"He's leaving all of his money to charity?"

"This adds a whole new wrinkle to the case. That widens the net even further. Either someone read the new will and got their revenge, or someone who didn't know it had changed thought they were going to benefit and didn't realize they were too late."

"We need to see a copy of the old will," I said, wincing as Bernie's claws dug into my leg.

"I'll contact the law firm first thing in the morning. In the meantime, we need to go through this dossier and talk to the butler."

Zane rapped once on the door before opening it and allowing an ashen faced Reginald to enter. Zane stood near the bookcase while Reginald took a seat next to me.

"Mr. Matthews said you wanted to interview me first?" Reginald said, licking his lips as he looked between Dave and me.

"Yes. When we came in here, we found a letter to Brynn written by the deceased. Were you aware of that?"

Reginald shook his head, his white hair shining in the light.

"I didn't. I knew something was going on, but Mr. Graff refused to divulge much to me."

"It says you witnessed a new will he had drawn up yesterday."

Reginald's head bobbed once.

"That's why I wasn't able to help you yesterday. Miss. Mr. Graff phoned and asked me to meet him in town at his attorney's office. It was most irregular."

"Did he say why he was taking this step?"

"No, but it wasn't my place to ask. He regularly changed his will, though. At least every two years. This isn't the first time he'd asked me to serve as a witness. It is something my family has done regularly in our years of service to the family. It's been an honor to serve Mr. Graff, and I look forward to serving the next."

Dave shared a look with me before leaning back in his chair and steepling his hands over his midsection.

"I don't think that will happen. According to this new will, the entire estate will be left to charity. The instructions state you are to oversee the transition and will be given a stipend to act as the executor."

Reginald went almost as white as his hair as Dave's words sunk in. He opened his mouth several times before finally speaking.

"What is to become of us, then? I've lived here my whole life. Mimi and I are well compensated, but we have little savings. Are we to be turned out on the street?"

His white face flushed red as his voice got louder, and I glanced over at Zane, noticing he was tensed, ready to spring into action if needed.

Dave cleared his throat and turned the page, continuing to read.

"I don't mean to upset you Mr... I'm sorry, I never got your last name."

"Miller. Reginald Miller Jr."

"Mr. Miller. The will continues that once your duties as executor are complete, you will be paid a final lump sum. From the amount I gather, you and your wife will live in relative comfort."

Bernie gripped my thigh with his claws again and I glanced down, startled. His green eyes blazed up at me and I tried desperately to read what he was trying to say to me.

"A lifetime of service, a family's lifetime of service, to end like this? It isn't right."

Reginald stood, knocking back his chair, and Zane walked forward, shoulders bunched. Dave lifted a hand and removed his reading glasses.

"There was more to the letter Mr. Graff left for Brynn. He said you were the only one he trusted, and he suspected that one of his family members was trying to kill him. Obviously, one of them did. Do you have any idea who he suspected?"

Reginald sat back down with a thump and raised a shaking hand to his hair, carefully patting it into place.

"I don't, I'm afraid. This has been so much to take in. I don't..."

The temperature in the room dipped and Dave looked around, startled. I tensed in my chair as Bernie's fur stood on end. The papers on the desk stirred, and I swore I heard a feminine laugh as the lights flickered before going back to normal. Dave gulped and looked at me, a question in his eyes. I shrugged and looked at Reginald, curious to see he was sitting, as if nothing had happened.

"Does that happen often?" I asked.

"Oh, yes. This old house is rather drafty. There must be a storm brewing outside," he said, face set into his familiar neutral expression.

He acted as though it was an everyday occurrence, but I remembered his warning the first day I'd come to this house. He knew more than he was saying. Bernie hopped down from the chair and melted into the shadows. Zane cleared his throat and nodded at Reginald.

"You were saying you don't know who would have had a motive to kill Mr. Graff?" he asked.

"Right. No. If Mr. Graff had any suspicions, he certainly never shared them with me."

"Could you detail your actions tonight, starting from when you brought Mr. Graff his drink?"

"Certainly. Every night before dinner, Mr. Graff had a vermouth with a single olive. It was his ritual when he was at home. I walked to the kitchen, where Mimi had the drink ready for me. I took it into the den, where Cynthia stopped me and took the drink from me. After that, I returned to the kitchen to check on the dinner preparations."

"I see. No one stopped you on the way? Nothing appeared wrong with the drink?"

He paused before answering.

"No, sir. I saw no one. I went directly from the kitchen to the den."

"I may have further questions for you, but I need to get statements from the family members. Has Stephen returned?" Dave asked.

Reginald shook his head as he stood and smoothed out his jacket, adjusting his cuffs.

"He hadn't returned while I was with the family. Shall I bring them to you one by one?"

"Please. I'll start with Robert."

"The elder or younger?"

"The elder," Dave said, rolling his eyes. "This family is something else. How do you keep them all straight?"

"It's a common trait among the wealthy, sir. Passing names on, and all that. I'll bring him to you directly."

Reginald bowed stiffly and exited the room, leaving a hush behind. Zane cleared his throat again as he took a seat next to me.

"Do you want us present while you interview everyone?" I asked. "I don't want to step on your toes."

Dave leaned forward over the desk and picked up the dossier, holding it out for me.

"Well, since the deceased obviously wanted you to investigate, who am I to say no? You can take this and read through it while I talk to them. I'll have you sit over there, if that's fine with you," he said, pointing to the wing chairs by the window.

I nodded as I took the file and stood.

"If I have a question, I might break in. Is that okay?"

"May as well. It's going to be a long night. I can't make heads or tails of these people so far. What did you think of the butler? And what was that breeze that ripped through here?"

Zane followed me to the wing chairs as I scanned the room for Bernie. He hadn't reappeared, and I was worried about him. Whoever that ghost was, she didn't seem friendly.

"I believe that was one of the two ghosts who is in residence. I haven't properly met her yet. The other is Cornelius Graff. He's Mr. Graff's grandfather. He was present when Stephen died. I have had little time to talk to him and discern why he's still here. As for Reginald, he seemed different. I don't know him well, but he seemed so angry. Zane, what did you think?"

"I think we need to see the old will before I comment. Something is off there. Before, I wouldn't have said I doubted him, but now? I'm just not sure."

The door swung open as we took our seats in the wing chairs. I put the dossier on my lap and scanned through it, wishing I'd had more time to prepare. Robert walked in behind the butler, hands crammed into his pant's pockets. He glared at Dave as if he was an interloper.

"I hope this will be quick. My wife is most upset, and we'd like to get out of this Godforsaken place. What are these two doing here?"

"Never mind them. They are here as consultants at a special request. Please, take a seat," Dave said, leaning back in his chair again.

"That's highly irregular. According to my sister, that girl was the one who killed my father."

THE DEMON IN THE DEN

"Why would she do something like that?" Dave asked.

Reginald bowed slightly and headed out of the room, closing the door with a soft click. Robert lowered himself into a chair, and I noticed the startling resemblance he shared with Cornelius Graff again. I wished the ghost would make a reappearance for these interviews.

"Who knows? I'm sure she thought she had something to gain. Although my sister is out of her mind on a good day, so I suppose whatever she said can be taken with a grain of salt. If you ask me, the old man keeled over from a heart attack. Not that he had an actual heart, but I assume there was some sort of organ in that chest. I wasn't in the room when my father passed, so I'm not sure how much help I can be. What do you want to know?"

"We'll start with the basics," Dave said. "Why you're here, your place in the family, and all that?"

I found Robert's name in the dossier and started reading, hoping Zane was paying attention and could fill me in later.

*a*s Robert droned on about himself, his family, and how he'd known this reunion was a terrible idea, I read what his father had to say about him. It wasn't a glowing report. There was little love lost between father and son, and very little respect. I perked up as Dave asked Robert what he'd meant when he'd knelt by the body.

"You were overheard saying that too many things were left unsaid once you found your father dead. Would you care to elaborate on that?"

"Ah, trying to save your own skin by tossing me under the bus, eh?" Robert asked, raising his eyebrow as he looked at me. "I meant nothing by it. Just that we'd had some words earlier in the day and it was too bad we'd never have time to come to an agreement. That's all."

"If you'll excuse my asking, it doesn't seem like you are overly upset by your father's passing."

Robert raised an elegant shoulder and waved off Dave's question, just like his father would have. I felt a momentary pang that Stephen Graff felt so beset by his family. The only people he could rely on were his butler and someone he'd hired a few days ago.

"We all have to go sometime. Father was getting up there."

"You mentioned arguing earlier in the day," I said, breaking into the conversation. "What was the argument about?"

I knew the chances of him owning up to what had been said were small, but I hoped maybe he'd let a hint drop unknowingly.

Robert cocked his head to the side and examined his fingernails.

"Recently, my father made, shall we say, some odd financial decisions. Honestly, I thought he was going senile. We had a few words, and that was that."

I watched the back of Dave's head, wishing I could see his face. A chill behind me raised the hair on the back of my neck and I heard Cornelius' familiar voice.

"He's lying. I overheard them and that was not the conversation."

I nodded slightly to show him I'd heard him. Zane looked at me and I blinked hard, hoping he'd get my unspoken message.

"Where did you go when you left the den?" Zane asked.

Robert stopped examining his hands and looked at us.

"The little boy's room. I met Eugene, and we talked about this farce before heading back to the den of vipers. See what I did there?" he asked, chuckling at his own joke.

"Eugene?"

"That's Cindy's husband. He's a saint of a man to put up with my wretched sister. And their terrible children."

"Can you think of anyone in your family who would want to end your father's life?"

Robert smirked and went back to looking at his fingernails.

"Would want to end, or would actually have the guts to do the deed? There's a difference, you know. My father was... difficult. I don't believe I'd ever actually wished the old man harm, but we didn't like each other. There was no friendly father and son banter with us. As for everyone else? Who knows? Anything is possible. If that's all? I need a smoke."

He stood, not waiting for Dave to answer, and headed for the door.

"Before you go, just one more question," Dave said. "What are your plans now that your father is gone?"

Robert paused, visibly irritated.

"I'll take over the reins, I suspect. That was always the plan."

"He's lying again," Cornelius whispered.

Zane looked over in my direction as I gripped the arms of my chair. I shook my head slightly, wishing I could say something.

Reginald popped his head in as Robert left.

"Who would you like next?"

"Robert's wife," Dave said, glancing down at the desk. "Lucinda."

"Right away, sir."

After he'd left, Zane and I joined Dave at the desk and I quickly relayed what Cornelius said.

"I thought something was going on," Zane said, rubbing my back. "Your face changed, and I thought I felt a little cold."

"Well, it's not surprising he was lying, but it would be helpful to know what exactly was said. Can you ask your ghostly eavesdropper for more information?"

"I never eavesdrop," Cornelius said right in my ear.

"He says he never eavesdrops. I'll ask him as soon as the coast is clear."

Zane and I took our seats as Reginald ushered Lucinda into the room with her two children in tow.

"I would like to get this over as quickly as possible," she said, sitting straight-backed in the chair and tucking her legs underneath it. "I also insist on being present when you interview my children."

"I don't have a problem with that. Minors should always have an adult present during a police interview. How old are they, ma'am?"

Robert Jr. and Sophie looked up from their phones and Sophia answered.

"We're twenty-two. We're twins."

Zane and I shared a look. This family was bizarre. They treated their adult children like toddlers incapable of independent thought. Although, after observing all four of the Graff grandchildren, maybe there was a reason.

"Okay," Dave said, drawing out the word. "Mrs. Graff, can you tell me what you observed in the den this evening?"

She nodded and relayed her impressions, which were shockingly close to what I'd seen. I'd expected her to take Cynthia's side and accuse me, but she surprised me by sticking close to the facts.

"Honestly, I agree with my husband. My father-in-law probably had a heart attack. I really don't think all of this interrogation is necessary."

Dave raised his shoulders before turning to the twins.

"What did you observe?"

Sophia put her phone down in her lap and smiled prettily at him.

"I'm sorry. I really wasn't paying attention. These gatherings are so dull. I've been talking with my boyfriend all night. Mumsie said I couldn't bring him and we hate to be separated."

"You said you were texting Stephen?" I asked.

She nodded and flipped her shiny hair over her shoulder.

"As soon as Granddad keeled over, I texted him when I saw he wasn't in the room. He said he'd run into town for something and would be back soon. He should be here any minute."

I looked over at Zane, shocked at her callous words about her grandfather.

"How about you, Robert?" Dave asked, watching the other twin, who was still engrossed in his device.

"He saw nothing," Sophia said, placing her hand on her brother's arm.

"I'm sorry, miss, but I was asking him."

Robert looked up, his handsome face blank, and shrugged.

"No."

And with that single syllable uttered, he returned his attention to his phone.

"May we be excused?" Lucinda asked, standing, her back straight as an arrow. "We'd like to retire for the evening. I didn't want to stay in this house, but I expect it's too late to get a decent room in town."

"You may go, but I'm asking everyone to remain in the house until the crime scene is cleared."

She snapped her fingers and her children followed her, disappearing as the door swung shut behind them.

"What's wrong with those kids?" Dave asked, turning to me.

"I'm not sure. Mimi mentioned the children liked to play pranks, but so far, I've only seen that from Stephen and Stephanie. Maybe these two grew out of that phase."

Reginald entered the room, carrying a tray that smelled delightful.

"I hope you don't mind, sir, but I have provided refreshments. I'm sure you're all famished. The family is rioting in the dining room, and I thought it best to feed them as well."

"Thank you, that was thoughtful. If you'll give us fifteen minutes before you bring in the next Graff? I'd like to see Eugene next."

"Of course."

Zane and I approached the desk like starving velociraptors as soon as Reginald was gone. There were three giant sandwiches piled on the tray next to a pot of tea. I grabbed one and took a big bite before Zane could stop me.

"Wait! Do you think it's safe? I mean, I know Mr. Graff said we could trust Reginald, but can we really? What if this is poisoned?"

I paused in mid-chew, suddenly realizing he was completely right.

"Well, I guess if Brynn doesn't kick over in the next few seconds, we'll know for sure," Dave said, eyes twinkling.

I swallowed hard and gave him a weak smile.

"Thanks for that. It tastes great if that means anything. I don't think Reginald would poison us. I mean, if he did, he'd have to explain away four bodies instead of just one."

Zane looked at my face, clearly worried.

"Are you sure?"

"It tastes exactly like the roast beef Mimi made before. I think it's okay."

He continued to watch me like a bomb about to go off, but finally nodded.

"If you feel anything strange, tell me immediately."

"Will do," I said, taking another bite, willing to risk it. "I guess if I go, this is one heck of a last meal. I really need to get that recipe from Mimi."

I set aside a piece of meat out of habit, hoping Bernie would return. He usually never failed to appear when there was food.

"Speaking of Mimi," Dave asked, in between bites of his own sandwich. "Do you think she's the guilty party? She's the one who made the drink, according to Reginald."

I thought about his question and shook my head.

"I don't think she would. She seems wonderful. Like a grandma. I don't think she'd do it."

"It's always the ones you least suspect. Maybe in this case, instead of the butler doing it, it was the butler's wife."

"My money's on Cynthia," Zane said. "I think she had Stephanie distract everyone with that loud noise and she dropped something in her father's drink. There has to be a reason she's so hell bent on blaming Brynn."

"Good instincts. I'll be interviewing her next. Let's finish this up and see what her husband has to say."

"I've never actually heard him talk," I said, before polishing off the rest of my sandwich.

Zane looked at his watch and then around the room.

"We have a few minutes. Do you think Cornelius is still around? This would be a great time to ask him some questions."

I glanced around the room, but could see nothing.

"Cornelius? Are you still here?"

I waited, but if he was still hanging around, he didn't respond. I shook my head at Dave as Bernie picked that moment to re-appear, his green eyes gleaming.

"I don't suppose you saved me anything?" he asked.

"Hey, cat," I said, wishing Dave knew about my ability to communicate with my cat. "Here you go, bud. I wish you'd been here earlier. You could have made sure it was safe to eat."

Bernie purred loudly as I handed him the meat, but I noticed he sniffed it carefully before swallowing it whole. Zane knelt next to him with another piece that also went down the hatch. Whatever Bernie was doing, he'd worked up an appetite.

"He almost seems like he's talking to you," Dave said, watching us keenly.

I gave a little shrug and reached for the tray, grabbing a napkin to wipe my hands.

"He's talkative, that's for sure. I'm ready whenever you are. If Cornelius shows back up, I'll try to question him if I can."

I went back to my chair and took a seat as Bernie jumped up next to me and curled into my side. Zane took my hand as he sat and squeezed it, smiling at me.

Regular as a clock, Reginald poked his head in again.

"If you're ready, I have Mr. Eugene here," he said.

Dave waved the man in and Eugene entered, looking sheepish as he took a seat. I wondered if that was his permanent expression. He shifted around and nodded at us.

"Could I have your full name?" Dave asked, once Eugene looked settled.

"Yes, it's Eugene Randall. Cindy briefly wanted me to change my name when we married. She wanted to remain a Graff, but my family wouldn't hear of it."

"I see. Please tell me what your movements were this evening before the death of Mr. Graff? You were seen leaving the den shortly before it happened."

"Of course," Eugene said. "I needed a little air. These family dinners are stressful and my ulcer is flaring up. I find taking brief breaks helps me feel better."

I wondered if his ulcer was named Cynthia, but held my tongue.

"Where did you go?"

"I walked the halls for a few minutes. You did a lovely job restyling the place," he said, smiling at me. "I like to admire the paintings when I'm alone. It's very peaceful."

"What happened then?"

"I ran into Robert and we walked back to the den. I was shocked to see my wife in such a state and her father on the ground. Do you know what happened to him? The man was in excellent health. I can't imagine him dropping dead suddenly."

"No, we'll need to wait for the coroner's report. Did you see anything strange on your way back into the den?"

Eugene startled for a minute and then settled himself back into the chair.

"No, I'm afraid not. I'm sorry I can't be of more help," he said, spreading his hands. "I simply left to clear my head. I saw my son go out the door, but I assumed he'd forgotten something in our car and would be right back. When I returned to the den, it was utter chaos. Cynthia is distraught. You'll have to excuse her outburst. I don't know what's come over her. I'm sure the young lady behind you would never hurt someone."

Dave looked over his shoulder at us to see if we had anything to ask. I couldn't think of anything pertinent, and Zane shook his head as well.

"Okay, Mr. Randall. That's all for now."

"Oh, my son has returned. Would you like me to send him in? Silly boy. I don't know what possessed him to leave like that."

My head came up as I heard his words and my eyes narrowed. I definitely wanted to know what Stephen had to say.

"Yes, please. I'm glad to hear I don't need to put out an A.P.B. for him. I'll interview Cynthia after him."

Eugene swallowed hard, his throat bobbing as he stood.

"I'm sure there's a reasonable explanation, Sheriff. I'll send him in. He's a rambunctious one, but he's harmless."

Dave waited until Eugene left before turning towards us.

"What do you make of that?"

"I think he's telling the truth, or at least the truth as he perceives it," I said. "I don't think he's like the others. He reminds me of an apologetic doormat who says sorry every time someone steps on him."

Zane snorted and laughed into his hand as Dave chuckled.

"Well, let's see what Stephen the younger has to say for himself."

12

Stephen walked into the room, strangely quiet, and took a seat. Instead of his typical quirky smile, he looked drawn, which surprised me. Out of all the relatives, I'd expected him to react to his grandfather's death with carelessness. Maybe there was something more to this kid.

"Stephen, correct?" Dave asked after several moments of silence.

"Yes, sir. I'm sorry I left. A buddy of mine texted me and asked to meet up for something. As soon as I heard what happened, I came right back. I never imagined something like this would happen," he said, looking towards the window and noticing us. "Why are they here?"

Dave glanced over his shoulder at us before looking back at Stephen.

"They're here as special consultants. They also witnessed what we believe to be the murder of your grandfather."

Stephen made eye contact with me before speaking.

"Was it bad?"

I nodded, unsure of what to say. He sighed and put his hands on the arm of his chair.

"I'm going to miss him. I know everyone else has their hands out and somersaults over each other, hoping to get featured in the will, but I actually loved him. Do you know who did it? I mean, it had to be one of us, right?"

"It looks that way. We have several suspects, and I'm afraid, son, you're on the list, especially since you left right before it happened. Did you put something in his drink and not want to hang around to see how it played out?"

I raised my eyebrows, surprised at Dave's tone. Stephen shook his head, face drawn.

"No. I couldn't do something like that, not to him. Look, I know it looks bad, but I can prove I was meeting my friend. I've got texts and everything. I just needed to get out of this place. My mom had been drinking, and well, you've seen how she is. The thought of sitting through another family dinner with her salivating all over herself to get my granddad's attention. I just couldn't handle it. I knew he would have understood."

"Were you and your sister named after him?"

Stephen's smile quirked on his face briefly before falling.

"Yeah, it's pretty obvious, huh? I think she thought she'd get a bigger chunk of the estate if she did that. As far as I could tell, it didn't help. She wanted to be the one to run things when he died, and she'd do anything to win one over Robert, my uncle. And I mean anything," he said, leveling a look at the sheriff.

"Why do you play pranks?" I asked, unable to sit quietly any longer. "No offense. It might have been cute when you were younger, but all of you are adults now."

He spread his hands and shrugged.

"Sorry about that. I guess it's an old habit. I can't stand being cooped up with my mom, and it's how I deal with it. My sister plays along, probably for the same reasons. You don't know what it's like."

Zane caught my eye, and I nodded. Somehow, the silly prankster was winning me over. He certainly seemed honest, and I couldn't blame him, I guess. If Cynthia was my mother, I'd probably act out, too.

"Do you know what you're getting in the will?"

Stephen nodded.

"Probably nothing, which is fine. Granddad set up a trust for me and my sister that's separate. I'll reach my majority next year and I can finally move out of the house and do my thing. I expected nothing. I just enjoyed spending time with him. He had the best stories. I can't even fathom I won't be able to come in here and talk to him anymore," he said, looking around the office. "This was his sanctuary."

The doors slammed open and Cynthia strode in, dragging Stephanie behind her. She looked like the figurehead of a ship as she stood there, chest heaving and eyes blazing.

"I demand to know why you are interrogating my son without me being present. Stephen, what have you told them?"

"Nothing, mom. Relax, it's not a big deal. I was explaining where I was."

"I will not relax. Why is that murderer here? This is highly irregular."

"Actually, it's not. Her presence was specifically requested," Dave said, standing. "And your son isn't a minor."

"I don't care. I must be present. I want her out of here and I want her out right now! My lawyer is on his way here right now. I had to get the lazy sot out of the bar to come here."

"You probably shouldn't say that in front of a peace officer," Dave said, tilting his head.

"I don't care what you are. Stephen, do not say one more word until Bertram gets here. This interview is over. If you want any of my cooperation, you'll get that woman out of here," she said, pointing at me.

Her volume increased to the point of hurting my ears. Zane stood and walked towards the desk.

"You need to lower your voice."

I joined him at the desk, dossier and envelope gripped against my chest, and looked at Dave.

"We can go. I'll continue going through this and we can talk in the morning," I said, desperate to defuse the tension in the room.

Dave regarded me before giving a sharp nod.

"That might be for the best. Drive carefully."

Zane took my arm as we walked past Cynthia and I gave her a wide berth. Stephen gave me an apologetic smile, reminding me of his father, and I wondered how everyone put up with the woman daily.

Reginald was just outside the door, and I wondered how easy it was to listen through the thick wood.

"You're leaving?" he asked, falling into step with us.

"Yes. I'll probably be back tomorrow. Thank you for that meal. That was very kind."

We stopped at the front door and I looked around the dim entry, hoping to spot Bernie. My bare arms prickled with gooseflesh as the light flickered again. Reginald's face blanched, and he opened the door quickly.

"See you then," he said, ushering us outside and closing the doors.

"Well, that wasn't weird at all."

Zane put his arm around me as we walked to the Jeep. I felt drained as the events of the night caught up with me.

"This has got to be the weirdest case I've ever been on. What do you make of everything? And where is Bernie? I can't leave him here."

He opened the door for me and Bernie appeared out of the underbrush at the side of the driveway.

"I thought you two would never leave," he said as he hopped in and jumped in the backseat.

I shook my head as Zane grinned at Bernie's antics.

"Never a dull moment," he said before closing the door.

On the drive home, we discussed what we'd seen, and I tried to get Bernie to tell me more about what he'd been doing, but he was quiet, refusing to answer. Zane walked me inside and Bernie streaked in, heading for the kitchen.

"I'm sorry our fancy dress-up evening turned out like this," Zane said, taking me in his arms. "You look so beautiful."

"And you're the handsomest man I've ever seen," I said, leaning into his broad chest. "I'm sorry, too."

"Get some rest, and we'll regroup tomorrow. I know Mr. Graff said he wanted you to investigate, but I want to help, too."

I nodded and held him close. Zane kissed me slowly before giving me a wry smile.

"One of these days, you're going to stay the night," I said, leaning against the doorframe.

"And when that happens, it will be amazing. You're tired and you've been through a lot. You need to sleep."

His grin meant sleeping wouldn't be on the menu if he stayed, and I reluctantly nodded. I was tired, even though my mind didn't want to quit.

"See you tomorrow, then."

He kissed me on the forehead before leaving, and I shut the door, spinning around to see Bernie at my feet.

"We're not sleeping just yet," he said, lashing his tail.

I groaned as I slipped out of my high heels and rubbed my feet.

"What do you mean? I'm exhausted, and everything is jumbled in my head. Maybe it will make more sense in the morning."

He rubbed his side on my leg and spoke more gently.

"I mean, we have one more thing to do. I need answers fast, and there's only one person who can give them to us. Tonight is a good night to see him."

"Who do you mean?"

"Your good friend, Charles Thurgood. We need to get moving. Go get changed and let's go. Unless you want to keep wearing that dress. Up to you."

He loaded himself into his carrier and picked at the lining with his claws, impatience clear on his black, furry face.

I dragged my feet back to my bedroom and changed into a pair of yoga pants and a tee. Bernie had a point. Nighttime was the easiest time for us to talk to Charles, a ghost who'd taken up residence in the local care home. It was a busy facility during the day, and I couldn't risk trying to contact him when everyone was around. He'd been a ghost for so long, he'd developed stronger powers and could manifest in the parking lot, where I could park at night without being seen.

"This had better be worth it," I said, grumbling under my breath as I walked back out to the living room.

"It will be. We need to hurry. Our window is closing."

I grabbed his bag and hopped in my car, heading for the care home as quickly as I could. I pulled into my usual place in the parking lot and turned off the engine before letting Bernie out of his bag.

"How does this work, exactly? The last time I was here, I was pretty sure you were the one who called Charles, even though I was trying to."

"Shhh. I'm concentrating," Bernie said, cracking one eye open before closing it again.

"Fine."

I drummed my fingers on the steering wheel and wished I knew how to call ghosts myself. That would make my job a lot easier.

"Good evening, my dear. You're looking beautiful as always," Charles said, appearing in the back seat. "It's been far too long."

I couldn't help but smile as I saw my ghostly friend. His dapper form hadn't changed a bit, and his face was lit with a grin.

"Hi Charles. I hope we didn't disturb you. Have you been pestering the intern nurses again?"

His mobile face pulled into a frown briefly before clearing.

"I know I shouldn't, but I can't help myself. The new one, Greg, is so easy to tease. I just move a few things around, nothing too major."

Charles, much like Ned, had developed a way of interacting with the physical world. Typically, ghosts couldn't move anything in our environment. I wondered how he did it, but that was a question for a different night.

"I'm sorry. I only visit you when I need something," I said. "But would you know anything about the Graffs? I think Cornelius was around during your time."

Charles nodded and adjusted his smart tie.

"Yes, my sweet, I knew him. We called him Old Corny, something he hated with a passion."

I giggled, picturing the dour Cornelius being saddled with such a ridiculous nickname. It served him right.

"Did you know his wife?" Bernie asked. "It's important."

"He talks?" Charles asked, eyes goggling.

"You can hear him, too? This is a new thing with him and I thought only I could hear him. I'm sorry he's being rude," I said, glaring at my cat.

Bernie heaved a sigh and shot me a look.

"Not now. Did you know his wife? We have little time."

Charles looked at the cat with a bemused expression and nodded slowly.

"I knew Mary Helen. She was, well, she was an interesting woman. In the twenties, women were finally coming out of their shells, as society loosened its restraints on them. Smoking in public, drinking, that sort of thing. Mary Helen embraced it wholeheartedly. In fact, during prohibition, she set up a still."

"She was a bootlegger?"

"She was. Cornelius, of course, did not approve. He didn't approve of her in the slightest, but she was the one with the money, you see. If Mary Helen wanted to make whiskey, that was precisely what she did."

"Could you describe her?" Bernie asked, breaking in.

"Well, she had dark hair and lively blue eyes. Tall and thin. Not what you would call beautiful, but we had a term back then for someone like her. She was a handsome woman. Forceful and strong. Do you know what I mean?"

Bernie nodded absently.

"That's her."

"Why the interest in Mary Helen? Or is it okay if I ask that, Mr. Cat?" Charles asked, eyes twinkling.

Bernie didn't answer, so I jumped in.

"I think she's still around, so to speak. Cornelius is too. He wouldn't answer me when I asked about her."

Charles leaned forward.

"Theirs wasn't a love match. Some say when he died suddenly, she had a hand in it. It was never proven, but that was the talk back in the day."

"Really? How did he die?"

"They called it a heart attack, but the word on the street was that she poisoned him with her own whiskey. She died a few years later, falling down the stairs in a drunken stupor, and their son took over the family business until the laws changed. I passed on shortly after, so I'm afraid I can't be of more help with what he did with his life."

"Cornelius said he was a disappointment."

Charles laughed merrily, shaking his head.

"He would say something like that. Old Corny is still around. What a crazy world we live in! May I ask, my dear, why this is pertinent?"

I quickly explained what had happened earlier, while Charles listened, enthralled. He let out a whistle as I finished, and Bernie laid his ears back at the sound.

"It looks like history is repeating itself," I said, finishing my story. "I wonder what else I can dig up in the Graff's closets."

"If their heirs are anything like they were, you'll probably find a few interesting stories."

"Thank you, Charles, for helping me again."

"It's a delight. What else have you been up to? I so love hearing your stories. I'd like to know how this one here started talking."

I glanced at Bernie and he nodded before curling up into a ball on the seat, apparently satisfied with the information he'd gotten. I wasn't sure how it all connected, but I'd press him later, when we were alone. I spent the next half hour talking with Charles until he went fuzzy around the edges, signaling he was losing his hold on maintaining his form.

"Well, my dear, it's time for me to go. Maybe I'll have just enough left to go pester Greg again."

"Be good, Charles."

He waggled his eyebrows at me before slowly fading away. I

looked down at Bernie, who was sound asleep and debated waking him to put him back in his carrier. I didn't have the heart to move him, though, so I settled for driving slowly back home. After this brief excursion, I was definitely ready to curl up in bed and sleep. Tomorrow, I'd go visit my friend Sophie at the library and see what else I could dig up on the Graffs.

13

The next morning, I was up before my alarm, even though I didn't want to be. The past few days of getting up way too early must have rubbed off on my system, and I wasn't happy about it. I fed Bernie and made coffee as I thought about everything that had happened in the past twenty-four hours. It had been one heck of a ride and I didn't know how I was going to accomplish the task Stephen Graff set out for me.

I sipped my coffee and paged through the dossier Stephen left me. There were no smoking guns, but it was clear there wasn't any love lost in this family. Or respect. I wasn't sure who killed Stephen. Cynthia was my obvious first choice, but was it too obvious? If there was anything I'd learned over the past few months, the person you least suspect is often the murderer. Here, though, that would have meant Reginald, and I wasn't willing to go down that path. Not yet, anyway.

Bernie finished his meal and sat next to me, washing up. I debated fixing something for breakfast, but decided it wasn't worth the effort. Since I was up so early, I'd go into the library and hopefully be the first one in. I hadn't seen Sophie in a while, and I was looking forward to seeing what my old friend was up to. I got ready for the day and looked at Bernie, who was sunning on the couch.

"I can probably sneak you into the library if you want to come with me," I said. "We've done it before."

He picked up his head before laying it back down.

"I need to think. There's something about the ghost of Mary Helen that disturbs me and some quiet time may help it become clear.

"Okie dokie, artichokie," I said as I gathered up my things and stuffed them into a tote. "You look like you need some more sleep."

"Enough with the artichoke thing, that's getting old," he said, cracking an emerald eye and glaring, before closing it again.

"I'll have you know that's a classic."

He let out a sigh, and I took that as my hint to leave. The morning sun warmed me as I walked to my car. I held my face up to it, soaking in the rays. It wouldn't be long before winter had its grip firmly fastened around us and I wanted to take advantage of the warmth while I could.

By the time I pulled up to the library, there were still a few minutes to go before it officially opened, but I bet Sophie would let me in early. The fewer people around to hear what I had to say, the better, I thought as I walked up the sidewalk. I peeked through the window and spotted Sophie at the front desk, talking to the newest librarian, Stacia. I rapped on the window and Sophie's face brightened as she saw me.

Within seconds, she'd thrown the lock and ushered me in, bracelets clanging merrily as she walked with me to the front desk.

"What a pleasure to see you, Brynn. Something tells me from the look on your face, you're going to jazz up my day."

"I think jazz may actually be the perfect word to describe it. Let me tell you what I'm working on," I said, looking over my shoulder as she ushered us into the Dakota Room.

This was the spot that held all the historic information on our area, and it was the perfect place to start my search into Mary Helen and the rest of the Graffs' history. I quickly told Sophie what I'd seen and watched as her eyes grew bigger.

"This is straight out of a classic mystery novel," she said. "Oh, I just bet the butler did it."

"Reginald, the butler, is so nice, though. I'd hate it if he was the killer."

"Well, you can't let that stop you from investigating. What do we need to research?"

"I wanted to start with Cornelius and Mary Helen. There has to be a reason they're both still here. Even though he's not the nicest human being, I'd like to help him cross over. Mary Helen, too, if she's willing," I said, adding the female ghost as an afterthought.

"We certainly don't want another banshee situation," Sophie said with a shudder.

"That's the truth. Where should we start?"

"I think the newspaper archives are the perfect starting point. There might be a few historical books with information on the family, but we can move to those next."

"You're the boss."

As she searched for the sections we'd need, we talked about the library and how Stacia was doing in her new position.

"She's a natural, dear. It's so nice to have someone to talk to. I think she loves books even more than I do."

I gasped theatrically and winked at Sophie.

"I don't think that's possible. It's nice she's here. It means we can spend more time together when I visit."

"Isn't that the truth? Here we go. Let's divide it up as we usually do."

We spent the next half hour in silence as we read through the archives. My section turned out to be disappointing and revealed nothing that was pertinent to the case. It did, however, reinforce the fact that the Graffs were well-regarded, wealthy, and all-together very important people. I snorted as I finished my pile and stacked it all back together for Sophie.

"I found nothing. How about you?"

She flashed a quick smile as she gave me a little pile of papers to read through.

"I think I found a few things. I'm not sure how important they are, but it might be interesting."

I took the stack and started scanning through it. To my surprise, she'd handed me the gossip columns from that time period. They were written in the old style, with coded wording. One caught my eye.

Does MH know the corn isn't always greener on the other side? If she's not careful, everyone will know her little secret.

"Sophie, what do you make of this?" I asked, holding the sheet up for her.

"It sounds to me like Mary Helen was having an affair and it was close to being public knowledge. Oh, I wish I could find out who wrote these old columns. Whoever did it was only active for a few years, but they are a hoot."

"Did you find anything else?"

"Just this one. I don't understand it, but maybe you will," she said before reading it aloud. "It says, 'Does father always know best? This son of a local family might disagree. Will he take over the family fortunes before his time?' I'm not positive this is the Graffs, but something tells me it's important."

I took the paper from her and re-read the section. It was much more vague than the other entry, but I agreed with my friend. Something about it felt right. Cornelius mentioned his son had a spending problem. Was it possible he'd attempted to take over the family business?

"What else did you find?"

She pointed out an obituary for Cornelius, and I read it quietly, feeling slightly disoriented. It was always weird to read about someone's death when you just talked to their ghost a few hours before.

"It says the cause of his death resulted from a sudden illness. I suppose back then, they didn't really do autopsies, huh?"

"If the family didn't want it done, they would've been able to block it," Sophie said. "I found Mary Helen's obituary as well. It says she died because of a fall. There's no mention in the news sections of either of their deaths, just the obits."

She closed the paper and carefully stacked it with the others on our table. I'd been hoping for a smoking gun that would have laid out exactly what happened, but this fell short. At least it confirmed what Charles said, and that was more to go on than I had the night before.

"Who do you think did it, Sophie?"

She stopped straightening the papers and looked at me, eyes bright.

"Well, if it's not the butler, it stands to reason it's who had the most to gain from Stephen's death. You need a copy of the old will, dear, and I think the pieces will fall into place."

"I should check with the Sheriff. Maybe he's already gotten that. Thank you for your help, Sophie."

I helped her put everything back, and we switched to happier topics as we worked. It felt good to catch up with her, and it brought me back to my childhood when she'd taken me under her wing. By the time we were done, I felt more centered and ready to keep digging.

"You'll have to let me know how it all turns out," she said as we walked back to the front. "I love hearing about your cases. If anyone can solve this convoluted case, it's you. I might go through some of the old books we have, too, and see if I can find anything else that is helpful."

"Thanks, Sophie. You're the most encouraging, efficient, and..."

"Effervescent?" Sophie asked, finishing our ritual word game.

"I love it! The most effervescent helper on earth."

She gathered me into a hug and I squeezed her tightly.

"See you soon, Brynn. I'll call if I discover anything."

"Thanks, Sophie. Bye, Stacia."

I walked back out into the sunshine and thought of my next move. It was almost lunchtime and if I wanted to talk to Dave, that meant tracking him down at Jill's cafe. The two of them were dating, something that filled me with joy and made my inner matchmaker bow gracefully. Jill had never married, and Dave's wife had passed away several years ago. They were perfect for each other. It didn't hurt that Jill served up some of the best food in the area, either. My stomach rumbled, reminding me I'd skipped breakfast as I hopped in my car for the short drive to the cafe.

My phone dinged with a text as I parked and I smiled as I saw Zane's message. I dialed his number as I turned off my car.

"Good morning, beautiful. Or I guess it's a good afternoon now. Did you get some sleep?"

"A little. Bernie had a mission for me after you left and we went to see Charles at the care home. He was very helpful."

I told Zane about my talk with Charles and what I'd learned at the library. He listened quietly and I could hear his gears turning.

"That is very interesting. Isn't it odd that a husband and wife are both ghosts in the same house and they don't communicate?"

"If Charles is right, and Mary Helen killed Cornelius, maybe not. I definitely need to get some answers. From both of them."

"Be careful. I've got to do a few things, but I can come over for dinner, if you'd like? My treat."

"I'd like it even if it wasn't your treat. I'll see what I can learn from Dave and maybe I'll swing by the Graff house, too. I can't wait to see what Cynthia's interview last night was like."

"Let me know what you find out. Love you."

"Love you, too. Later, Matthews."

"Later, Sullivan."

I got out of my car and walked in front of the cafe, smiling when I saw Dave seated in a booth, with Jill across from him. I couldn't wait to talk to the Sheriff and compare notes.

14

*J*ill popped up from the booth as soon as she saw me walk in and motioned for me to join them. I headed towards them, nodding at Kelly, the waitress who'd made it possible for Jill to slow down a little and enjoy life.

"Brynn! We were just talking about you," Jill said, sliding next to me as I got comfortable in the booth.

Dave was engrossed in his club sandwich and nodded at me before taking another bite.

"All good, I hope," I said with a wink. "What's the special today?"

"One of your dad's favorites, the patty melt. Do you want that, or your usual cheeseburger?"

"Ooo, that is always good. I'll go with that, but you don't need to rush off. I'm not in a hurry."

"You may be after this one here starts talking," Jill said, thumbing in Dave's direction. "I'll be right back."

She bustled off, shouting my order across the back counter to the cook before walking over to the soda machine. She knew me well. There was nothing I liked better than a Coke with my lunch.

"So, what's up?" I asked, waiting for Dave to finish chewing.

He pushed his upside down cowboy hat to the side and handed me a legal document. Score! He'd found Stephen Graff's prior will.

"What do you make of it?" he asked.

I took a second to read through the first page before letting out a whistle. Once Robert found out about the new will, he would not be a happy camper.

"This is interesting. In this version, Robert would have inherited most of the estate, as well as control of the family business. Cynthia wouldn't get much from the looks of it. Neither would the grandkids."

I put the document down and looked at Dave, curious to see what he was thinking. He took a long drink of his coffee and slid his plate to the side.

"What business are these folks in, anyway? It's not clear from the will what exactly they do."

"That's a good question. I learned Stephen's grandmother was a bootlegger. I wonder if they made it official. Let me see what I can find online."

I pulled out my phone and searched for Stephen Graff, pulling up a long list of results. While I read through the pages, Dave watched Jill as she interacted with customers. I peeked over the top of my phone, delighted to see the look of love in his eyes. He must have felt me watching him and glanced down, cheeks red.

"Find anything on that phone of yours?"

"Well, it looks like most of their wealth was from investments, and Stephen was on the board of several companies as an advisor. I'll have to keep digging, but from the first glance, it looks to be substantial. Can you pull his financial records?"

"Already got a call into the primary bank he used. His attorney gave them authorization to let me look at it. I'll know more in a few hours, I think."

Jill came back, holding a plate with her famous patty melt, heaped with fries. She barely had it in front of me before I picked up the sandwich and took an enormous bite. It was every bit as delicious as I'd remembered it being.

"Jill," I said, covering my mouth with my hand. "I don't know how you do it. You should write a recipe book."

"I don't know about that," she said, joining me in the booth. "But I appreciate it. How's your father doing, anyway?"

We spent a few minutes catching up, but my mind was on the business of Stephen Graff's will. What if one of his family members snuck into the office before he was killed and spotted the new will? Had they killed him out of spite? It just made little sense.

Once I had mopped up the last of my ketchup with a fry, I wiped my hands and went back to reading the will while Jill and Dave kept talking. I saw something that made me gasp, pulling their attention to me.

"What?" Dave said.

"I noticed that in this version, Reginald and his wife were allocated a lot of money. Like a lot."

I slid the papers over to Dave while my mind raced. Reginald had witnessed the will. Did he know what was in it? Had he gotten so angry he'd killed his employer to get even? In the newest version, he was to act as executor, and would get a stipend, but it was less than this number.

Jill looked between us before raising an eyebrow at me. I quickly described my theory to her, not wanting to believe it. Once I was done, she cocked her head to the side.

"Seems to me you shouldn't witness a will you're a beneficiary of. Or be the executor. I'm going off the memory of my old granny making a will, but that seems a little off to me."

Dave nodded as he took another sip of his coffee.

"You're right, dumpling," he said, glancing at me, and blushing. "I asked the attorney about that, and he said Stephen insisted. He was used to getting his way, and the attorney allowed it, since he's known them both for forever. Reginald didn't read the will in front of the attorney, but he signed it when instructed to. The other witness was a secretary for the firm. You've got a good point, Brynn."

"I hope he's not the one. What were you saying last night? What if it wasn't the butler, but his wife? Do you think that's possible? I mean, the drink was made in her kitchen."

I didn't want the killer to be Mimi or Reginald, but I had to admit, things were looking bad for the couple. They might have even worked together.

"It's possible. I interviewed her last. She had little to say, but she seemed angry under the surface, if you know what I mean. Reginald must have shared the new contents of the will with her."

"But Stephen said we could trust Reginald implicitly. It just doesn't feel right that the one person he trusted might have killed him."

"Stranger things have happened," Jill said. "Personally, I think the person who stood the most to gain is always the guilty party. If Robert didn't know he would not inherit, he might have bumped his father off."

"You may be right," Dave said, taking her hand in his.

"What about Cynthia?" I asked, half dreading hearing about her interview.

Dave grimaced before patting Jill's hand and leaning back into the booth. From his body language, it was obvious it hadn't gone well.

"By the time her high flying lawyer arrived from Rapid Falls, it was late. Once he was there, he kept advising her not to answer questions. It was a farce. I got little out of her besides the fact she thinks you did it."

"That's just horse pucky," Jill said, eyes narrowing. "I've known this girl my entire life and she wouldn't do such a thing. You better not tell me you're actually considering that."

Dave barked out a laugh and reached to grab his hat.

"Of course not. I've known her almost as long. Brynn is only wired to help people, not hurt them. All I know is Robert is taking his sister's advice to heart, and now he's lawyering up. I've asked them all to remain until the will is read, which is scheduled for tomorrow. I can't hold them past then, Brynn, so if you're going to solve this case, I suggest you move fast. Once they're gone, it's going to be that much harder. The will is going to be read at nine, so I'll need you to attend, if you can."

I nodded, determined to figure out this mystery.

"I'll be there. I'm going to head up to the Graff's house, if that's okay with you. I need to talk to a few people."

"It's fine with me, but watch your back. One of them is a murderer. I've asked the coroner to rush his autopsy and let me know the actual cause of death. I'll know something later today. The lab is also going to be in touch with the analysis of the contents of his glass. The den should still be cordoned off, but it's fine if you want to go in there. My team got everything they needed from there."

Jill patted my hand before letting me out of the booth. I tried to pay, but she waved off my cash. As soon as her back was turned, I folded it and placed it under my glass, before walking out of the cafe to my car. I briefly thought about swinging by my house to grab Bernie, but decided against it. As it was, by the time I made it to the house, and hopefully talked to Cornelius and Mary Helen, it would be late.

I turned up my music and sang along as I drove, happy to be out in the sunshine. I didn't know what I was going to run into at the Graffs, but for right now, it was a beautiful day and I was determined to enjoy it. I pulled up to the gate and was surprised that it didn't swing open as it normally did. I hit the button next to the speaker and waited for a few minutes before Reginald's voice crackled through it.

"Ah, hello Miss Sullivan. I'll buzz you in."

I drove up and parked, curious about the added security. Reginald was waiting for me at the door, and looked much better than he had the previous night.

"Hi, Reginald. Thanks for letting me in."

"I'm sorry for the delay. The sheriff asked me to screen and log all the visitors to the house. So far, you've been the only one. We've had the gate set to automatic for so long, I almost forgot about it."

"No worries. Do you mind if I go into the den? The Sheriff cleared me to enter. Is the family around?"

"Lunch was served an hour ago, and I believe everyone has retired to their quarters," he said, as he walked with me to the den.

"How's everyone doing?"

His jaw tightened, and he shook his head.

"The mood is dark. I believe everyone is out of sorts."

He turned to leave, but I put my hand on his arm to stop him.

"Reginald. What do you know about the ghosts here?"

He reeled around, looking at me like I had two heads. I was going out on a limb, but I'd noticed his reaction to the flickering lights, and I was convinced he knew more than he was saying.

"What do you mean?" he asked, straightening his tie.

"The cold drafts, the flickering lights, slamming doors. You know, the ghostly activity that happens, I'm guessing, daily. It's okay, Reginald. I'm familiar with ghosts."

He eyed me suspiciously and cleared his throat.

"Well, then. I see. I don't know what to say."

"I've met Cornelius."

I waited, hoping my bald statement would put him at ease. I knew how hard it was for some people to talk about ghosts. Heck, it was hard for me to talk about them, and I'd been communicating with them for years. It was only recently that I'd found my courage and my purpose, and had been willing to talk about my gifts. When he didn't answer, I pressed him.

"I also believe I've met Mary Helen. She's an interesting one, that's for sure."

Reginald's eyebrows flew up, and he nodded several times.

"Well, I guess that answers some questions I've had," he said, nervously looking around. "I kept trying to play it off, but it happens so often, you see. Footsteps up in the attic. Cold drafts when everything is sealed tight. I didn't realize there were two of them, though."

He looked so uncomfortable my heart went out to him. I patted his arm and smiled.

"It's okay. There are actually a lot more ghosts out there than people think. Most don't mean any harm."

I didn't want to talk about Mary Helen's abilities of slamming doors, figuring that would send him over the edge. I wasn't sure what kind of person she'd been in life, but in death, she was definitely odd. And apparently angry.

He let out a sigh and gave me a weak smile.

"I guess it's good to have confirmation. Do you actually see them?"

"I see them and I can communicate with them. Cornelius was actually here when Mr. Graff, well, passed. I was hoping to talk with him in the den. Do you mind keeping an eye out for the family? I'd prefer not being interrupted, if it's possible. It's rather awkward, talking to ghosts."

"I can only imagine. I will, of course, assist in any way I'm able. Do you need me to, uh, stay in the room with you?"

From his expression, I could tell that was the last thing he wanted to do.

"That won't be necessary. If you could stay in the dining room and alert me if anyone approaches, that will be just fine."

He nodded sharply.

"Excellent. If you require anything, I am only a shout away."

He walked away quickly, and I squared up my shoulders before stepping under the crime scene tape Dave's men put on the door. The den was just as it had been when I'd left it the night before, minus Mr. Graff's body, and there was an eerie calm to the room. I looked at the carpet, able to make out the stain where his vermouth had spilled.

"Have you solved the crime yet? Or are you more of a Watson than a Holmes?"

Cornelius' sour voice echoed through the room and I turned to see him, standing by a couch, arms crossed.

15

*H*is comment threw me for a loop for a second until I realized just how old the Holmes stories were. I hadn't expected him to be a fan of fiction. Cornelius glowered at me, drifting closer.

"I just realized those stories were in print when you were alive. I'd forgotten about that," I said. "What was your favorite case?"

"The Adventure of the Speckled Band. Have you read Doyle?"

"Yes, I'm a huge fan. I always liked The Dancing Men, myself."

"That was a good one," he said, nodding in approval. "I didn't realize you were a reader."

I was amused that we'd both misjudged each other. Much like I'd written Stephen the younger off as a young punk, maybe there was more to Cornelius than I'd expected. At least he'd thawed towards me and I felt the energy in the room change from discordant to, well, not pleasant, but much less oppressive.

"I love books, especially mysteries. It seems like we've got a complicated one on our hands here. And maybe even an old mystery?" I asked, crooking up an eyebrow.

Cornelius looked sharply at me, his dark eyes locking with mine. A shadow of a nod bent his head briefly and he floated closer.

"So, you're more than just a designer, I see."

"I try. Lately, it seems like I've been stumbling over murder mysteries left and right. You know, I can do more than talk to ghosts. I can, well, I can help them move over. When they're ready."

He looked at me with a shocked expression and his form started wavering. My heart leapt in my chest, and I worried he was about to disappear. I needed to ask him some questions, and I wasn't sure how long it would take him to generate enough energy to return, especially since I didn't have Bernie to assist me. I should have stopped and brought him with me. Luckily, the shock must have worn off quickly, since his form solidified.

"I see. How does that work exactly?"

"That's a good question, and I don't know if I have an appropriate answer. I think when a soul is left here, they have unfinished business. It's my job to help them complete that business, so they are no longer tethered here. When it's time, it just, well, it just kind of happens."

He floated around the room, brow furrowed, before looking over at me again.

"Do you know where a soul is going beforehand? I don't know that I'm a big believer in the afterlife, but it would be a cruel surprise to expect one place and end up in another. If that's the case for me, I'd rather remain."

I walked closer to him and shook my head, surprised to see genuine fear reflected in his eyes.

"I'm afraid I don't know that either. But I believe if wrongs were committed while you were alive, part of the reason your spirit ends up tethered here is to set things right."

His shoulders relaxed and while I wouldn't say he smiled, he unclenched a little.

"That's good to hear. Not that I'm worried about that, of course. I was an upstanding citizen while I was alive."

I shrugged, not wanting a theological discussion to derail my purpose. I didn't know how things were settled. When I'd helped souls cross over, I'd only experienced a wonderful feeling of bliss, and caught a few glimpses of something undefinable, but awe striking.

"Maybe you could assist me in solving this case. That could be why you're still here," I said, trying to get the conversation back on track. "Did you see anything? You were here when it happened, just like me."

Cornelius floated towards the liquor cabinet, eyeing the spot on the carpet just like I had.

"Nothing stood out. It's a shame Stephen went before his time, though. I could tell something bad was going to happen. Do you think he'll end up like me? How did you describe it? Tethered to this house?"

"It's possible, but I don't think it's likely. I think if he was still around, his soul would have shown up, just like yours. Did it take you a long time to manifest when you passed on?"

His eyebrows rose, and he looked at me strangely.

"You know, I honestly don't know the answer. I don't think it was a long time, but it's hard to tell. One minute I was alive, the next I was standing there trying to get people to notice me. It took me a while to realize I was dead."

I sat on the couch and thought about what I'd learned of his death, both by rumor and what had been in the paper. Did he know the truth?

"Your obituary said you passed after a sudden illness. Was that what happened?"

"You read my obituary?"

"Just earlier today. Don't worry, it only said nice things about you."

"As it should. I was a good person. I don't remember an illness, though. My last memories were of a dinner party with our friends and my son's family. My wife, Mary Helen, sat next to me. For once, we weren't arguing. I think that's why I remember it so clearly. After eating, I felt off and retired early. The next thing I knew, I was standing next to my bed, shouting at Arthur, my valet. He never heard me."

We made the connection at the same time and he floated closer to me. I looked at the spot on the rug and back at him.

"They say history repeats itself. Do you think you were poisoned?"

A shadow crossed his face and his eyes were grave as he shook his head.

"It's possible."

"Do you think it was Mary Helen?" I asked, knowing I was risking angering him, but pushing through.

To my surprise, he let out a snort.

"It wouldn't surprise me. We were always at each other with hammer and tongs. I never thought she would've killed me, though."

"Is that why she's still here, too?"

His face flushed, and he looked agitated as he started wavering around the edges.

"Don't speak of that."

"Why? I understand it would be awkward to share your house with someone you don't like while you're alive, let alone when you've both passed on, but surely you can talk at least. Work something out?"

His face was menacing as he swirled around me.

"She won't talk to me! Every time I approach her, she disappears, her laughter echoing. It's maddening, I tell you, maddening! I deserve to know what she's doing here!"

He was mostly transparent, and I knew I only had a few seconds before he disappeared.

"Where can I find her? Maybe she'll talk to me."

"Her sewing room is where I've glimpsed her the most. That dratted woman couldn't even have a normal room in the house for herself. She had to pick the basement!"

And with that shout, he disappeared, leaving me alone in the den. I pounded my fist on my thigh, irritated I hadn't gotten to ask as many questions as I wanted to. Now, not only did I have Stephen's murder to solve, but it looked like Charles Thurgood was right. Cornelius had been murdered, too. As much as I dreaded facing Mary Helen, it looked like that was going to be my best option for getting answers.

I left the den and found Reginald leaning against the door frame of the dining room, lost in thought. As soon as he saw me, he straightened, blushing bright red as he adjusted his tie.

"Forgive me, miss. I was taking a slight break while I waited."

"Don't worry about that. I'm sure your job is tiring. Would you know where the entrance to the basement is?"

His red color faded immediately, and I put my hand on his arm, concerned he was going to pass out.

"The basement? Why?"

"I need to see Mary Helen. Apparently, that's where she likes to hang out when she's not in the hallway."

His voice shook as he smoothed his white pompadour, looking like he'd rather be anywhere but here.

"I can show you. I should escort you down there, though. It's not in good condition and I'd hate for something to happen to you down there."

My heart went out to the older man.

"It will be fine. I've got a flashlight on my phone. I'll be careful. I don't expect you to go down there."

"I insist. Follow me please."

He put on his butler's face and strode ahead, leading me down the hall past Stephen's office. He finally came to a stop at the end of the wing and motioned towards a door before swallowing hard.

A voice rang out down the hall, making me cringe.

"Reginald! I need something. Now!"

Reginald licked his lips and looked at me before looking down the hall.

"Go ahead. I'll be fine. It shouldn't take me long. Go see to Cynthia. I'm sure she doesn't appreciate waiting."

"I said now!"

Her strident voice gained volume, and I decided a scary, dilapidated basement was better than running into her again. I opened the door and turned my flashlight app on, nodding encouragingly at Reginald.

"Go. I'll be fine."

His footsteps faded as he rushed down the hall and I looked down into the darkness below. Have I ever mentioned I hated basements? Well, I do. With a passion. I steeled myself as I headed down the stairs, walking as slowly as I could.

Once I was at the bottom, I looked around, hoping to find a light switch. Even though the house was old, other parts of the place had been modernized. There had to be electricity down here, right?

I found a wall and felt around, fumbling as I heard what sounded like a laugh coming from deeper in the basement. It sounded like Mary Helen was here, but would she appreciate me treading in her domain?

I steeled myself and kept searching for a switch, moving to another wall and feeling along it. Finally, my fingers connected with a round knob and I breathed a sigh of relief. I tried to turn it before remembering that houses in this era had push button switches. I pressed it and heard a welcome answering hum as the lights came on.

The basement wasn't much better in the dim light, but at least I could see where I was going. I walked further and spotted a room tucked away in the back. As I walked in, I couldn't help but laugh. When Cornelius said Mary Helen had a sewing room, I should have known it wasn't being used for that purpose. A huge still sat in the corner, its copper sides gone green with age.

"What's so funny?"

I whipped my head around, surprised to see Mary Helen standing next to me. Her eyes were narrowed, and she didn't look friendly.

"I should've known it wasn't actually a sewing room. I talked to Charles Thurgood, and he mentioned you were a bootlegger. I just didn't expect to see a still down here."

"Charlie? You talked to Charlie? How?"

She'd gone from angry to inquisitive in two seconds flat and I said a silent prayer of thanksgiving I'd mentioned my ghostly friend. From her expression, it was obvious she liked Charles.

"He's still around, much like you. He's currently haunting the care home that was built on top of the lot where his house used to be."

Her musical laugh filled the space, and for once, it didn't have the ominous tone I'd gotten used to hearing.

"Old Charlie. Isn't that a hoot? I wish I could leave this place. He was always such a card. He'd at least be fun to hang around with, unlike the old stick that I was stuck with."

I snorted before covering my mouth. Her lips quirked, and she raised a pencil thin eyebrow.

"I see you've met him, too. He's been dead for decades and he still hasn't loosened up. Cornelius and his blasted propriety. I've told him until he changes I won't talk to him, but does he listen? No, he just keeps hounding me. Even in death, I can't get away from that man."

I walked around the still, imagining what it looked like when it was new.

"Did you enjoy making whisky?"

She nodded and floated closer.

"I did. And I loved calling this my sewing room. I was never one for womanly pursuits, but this was something I was passionate about. If it hadn't been for that stupid prohibition law, I never would've discovered it. Are you the one with the black cat?"

My head went back, surprised at her change of subject.

"Yes, that's Bernie. He mentioned he'd seen you."

She rolled her eyes and took a long, elegant cigarette holder out of her pocket, twirling it in her fingers before looking at it ruefully.

"It stinks not being able to smoke any more. This whole being dead thing just stinks. Anyway, that cat is far too nosy."

"It's one of his best features," I said, unable to keep from defending him.

"Well, if that's his best feature, I'd hate to see his worst. Why are you here, anyway?"

I leveled with her, hoping her current state of goodwill would last as I described my mission from Stephen, her grandson. She nodded as I spoke, drifting around the room. I finally got to the question I really wanted to ask once I was done summing up what happened so far.

"Did you see if anyone poisoned the drink on its way to the den?"

Mary Helen shook her head ruefully, her bobbed hair flying.

"I was down here when I felt the shift. I knew someone was going to die, but I didn't think it would be Stephen. The old patterns are repeating."

"Shift? Patterns?"

"You don't know, do you? When a life leaves this house, you can feel it in its bones. I was worried you'd be the one to die, but I was wrong. I felt it before, see. Twice. Once before Cornelius died, and then again. As for the patterns, I guess I was the only one who really knew the truth."

"The truth about what?"

"Who killed Old Corny and then me? I know everyone thought I did away with him, but I didn't. As much as I didn't like him, a part of me still loved him. Who would've thought? It was an arranged marriage, you see. My father wanted me married to someone suitable, and he told me on my wedding day that we'd develop feelings for each other. Eventually. Too bad most of those feelings were bad. I did sort of love the old stick, though."

She rambled on while I waited impatiently for her to get to the point. Finally, I couldn't take it anymore.

"Who killed you?"

She stopped and turned towards me, eyebrows raised.

"My child, of course. That's what I meant by patterns."

My mind reeled as I put everything together.

"You think Robert or Cynthia..."

"It's certainly possible. Obviously, someone killed Stephen, and it wasn't you. Old Reggie doesn't have it in him to kill. Besides, history always repeats itself."

She let out a musical laugh and vanished abruptly, cutting off the lights as she went. I stood for a second, plunged into darkness, and cursed softly. Of all the ways to be dramatic, she had to pick turning off the lights. I groped for my phone and flipped on the flashlight before picking my way through the basement towards the stairs.

My mind swirled with questions as I walked back to the main level and looked around. I didn't see Reginald, and luckily, none of the Graffs were present as I went to the door. What I needed was a nice, relaxing night with Zane and Bernie. Maybe the three of us could put our heads together and make sense of everything.

16

I was deep in a dreamless state when I felt something cold touch my ear. Something like a cat's nose. Ripped from sleep, I flailed around on the bed, trying to make sense of where and who I was.

"Wha...? What's going on?"

"The reading of the will is at nine, right? Well, you've got about twenty minutes to feed me before Zane shows up," he said, stepping back and eyeing me doubtfully. "I think you're going to need all of that to tame your hair. I should have gotten you up sooner."

I groaned as I fell back onto my pillows. This was the first day I'd slept in and right now, I wasn't thinking very nice thoughts about the Graffs. Between the frustrating ghostly relations to the annoying ones who were alive, I was thoroughly sick of the family.

"I'm coming. I'm coming," I said, climbing out of bed and shuffling to the bathroom.

I did a double take when I spotted myself in the mirror. Bernie was right. I must have had some crazy dreams, based on how my hair was rioting around my head in a snarled cloud. I brushed my teeth, wrestled with my hair, and threw on some clean clothes before joining Bernie in the kitchen. He was practically running in place in front of the cupboards, so I made sure he had his food before even thinking about coffee. I checked my watch and sighed, knowing I wouldn't have enough time to get my coffee brewed before Zane showed up.

Our strategy session, held over some of our favorite delivery pizza, had stretched late into the night, and my mind still felt fuzzy. The only conclusion we could come to was Robert or Cynthia made the obvious choice as the murderer. It made sense, but how we were going to prove it? And which one did it?

We'd worked out a plan for after the will was read, and I could only hope everything would go as we wanted it to. If it didn't? I wasn't even sure what the answer was to that question. I heard Zane's Jeep pull up and Bernie finished swiping his tongue around his bowl before jogging into his bag.

"Let's go!"

I followed at a slower pace and opened the door, breaking into a smile when I saw Zane on the other side, holding to-go cups of coffee and a bag from Jill's Cafe that smelled delicious.

"You're my hero," I said, taking a coffee from the tray and gulping it down.

I didn't even care it was scalding hot. My tongue cared, but my brain told it to shut up and keep going. Zane chuckled and shook his head.

"That's my girl. Want to save time and eat on the way? I called Dave and told him what we came up with last night. He's going along with our idea and will be there as backup."

I grabbed Bernie's bag and zipped it before tossing the strap over my shoulder.

"Sounds good to me. Sorry, I slept in."

"You needed some sleep. I told Bernie not to wake you up too early. I'm still not sure I like the idea you came up with of antagonizing Robert and Cynthia. What if one of them hurts you?"

"It will be okay. I trust you."

I glanced at Bernie through the mesh and smiled when he winked at me. Even though he'd been snarky this morning, I knew they both cared. Somehow, I knew Bernie would do everything in his kitty power to protect me, and so would Zane.

We got settled in the Jeep and I took the bag, portioning out the breakfast sandwiches and hash browns. I inhaled the scent of the ham and cheese croissant and nearly groaned.

"Yep, you're my official hero."

We ate our breakfast in silence, and I slipped a little piece of cheese into Bernie's bag, knowing how much he enjoyed it. He bumped my finger with his nose before accepting his treat and chowing it down in seconds.

"Did you come up with any other theories after I left?" Zane asked, balling up his wrapper and tossing it in the bag at my feet.

"No. I think we're on the right track. We just have to hope that Robert, if he is guilty, shows his hand at the reading of the will. What will it be like? I've never been to one of these before. I've read about them, but something tells me real life will differ from how it's portrayed in books."

"I don't know either, but we're about to find out. Is Bernie coming inside with us?"

I glanced into the backseat, where Bernie was grooming himself, and raised an eyebrow. He stopped in mid-lick, heaving a sigh.

"Of course I'm going with you. This time, I want you to take me in the bag, but leave the zipper open a little so I can hop out if I need to. I don't enjoy being trapped in this thing."

I relayed his message to Zane and shrugged as I turned back around. I was sure Bernie had a reason behind his request, and honestly, it felt good knowing he was going to be near me.

This time, as we approached the house, the gate was sitting wide open. Seeing the camera mounted there reminded me of the security footage Zane wanted to see of the place the night Stephen Graff died.

"Did Dave say anything about the security footage?" I asked as he parked behind a shiny black car.

Zane grimaced as he turned off the engine.

"Yeah, I guess the footage wasn't useful, beyond confirming that the younger Stephen left before the drink was delivered and cleared him."

"Well, that's good, I guess. I wish they had a feed on the inside of the house. That would really make our lives easier."

"True. Are you ready for this?"

"As ready as I'm going to be."

I looped Bernie's bag over my shoulder and followed Zane up to the front door, thinking about how much had changed since the first time I'd pulled up to the place. I still had the check Stephen Graff had left me sitting on my kitchen table. Somehow, I didn't feel right about putting it in my account, especially since we hadn't solved his murder yet. Even if we did, I didn't know what I was going to do with it. I shook off my thoughts as the door swung open, revealing a somber Reginald.

"Good morning, you two. I thought you might have been lost in the basement yesterday, but I saw your car was gone."

"I'm sorry. I didn't know where you were and I didn't want to risk running into Cynthia."

"I understand completely. Everyone else has gathered in the den. Would you like to join them?"

I nodded and took Zane's hand as we followed the butler. It felt good to have

Zane's calming presence as we got closer to the room. As we entered, I suppressed a chuckle, wondering if this is where the saying a 'den of vipers' came from. The looks we got were certainly not friendly as we filed in.

"What is she doing here?" Cynthia said, her voice ringing out as usual.

Eugene gave me his characteristic embarrassed smile and nodded in our direction before mumbling something to his wife.

I ignored her question and instead focused on finding us a place to sit. Stephen jumped up from his place on the other couch and waved us over.

"You can sit here. I'm too wound up to sit, anyway. Steffie, move over."

His sister looked at us before inching towards Sophia. I tucked Bernie's bag under my legs as I sat, and Zane took the position next to the arm of the couch, deciding to stand. I glanced around the room, noting everyone was present, minus the lawyer. Robert refused to make eye contact, but glanced over at us briefly before sniffing loudly.

Movement at the door caught my eye, and I saw Reginald usher in a small, balding man. Behind them was Mimi, and she looked flushed and more uncomfortable than I was. I spotted Dave's cowboy hat in the middle of the doorway and relaxed a little. If he was here, he'd make sure no one was killed. Again. I hoped, anyway. The lawyer took a spot by the fireplace and nodded at everyone present.

"I see you're all here. I'll begin by reading the last will and testament of Stephen Graff. I would ask that you hold your questions until the reading of the will is complete."

Robert rubbed his hands together and gave his sister an evil smile before addressing the lawyer.

"Let's get this show on the road. We need to get back to our house, and I want to continue my father's legacy."

"Alright sir. As you wish."

The small man cleared his throat and began reading, only to be stopped by a shout from Robert after announcing the day the will had been made.

"What? That was only a few days ago? Are you telling me there's a new will?"

Cynthia smirked and leaned across Eugene, who sank back into the cushions.

"Too bad, brother. Things may not go your way. For once."

The lawyer cleared his throat again, and they fell silent. He droned on, going through the preliminaries, and I tensed my spine, knowing full well what was coming next. As soon as he got to the part about donating the entire estate to charity, all hell broke loose.

"This is outrageous. That is a forgery."

Robert paced the floor, ranting and raving. The veins in his neck were popping out and his face was flushed as red as I'd ever seen someone get. Cynthia was also on her feet, shrieking like a bird of prey. The lawyer's voice cracked like a whip, startling everyone.

The small man pulled himself up to his full height and lowered his glasses on his nose.

"I will not answer questions until the entire contents of the will have been read."

He kept reading aloud, ignoring the muttering and occasional shouts. I glanced at Zane, noticing how tense he was. His head was on a swivel, looking at everyone.

The lawyer finally stopped droning on and silence filled the room for a few seconds. Suddenly, it was as if a giant inhaled, and it felt like all the oxygen left the room.

"You mean to tell me that my father left more money to the stinking butler and cook than to me? His only daughter?"

Cynthia was on her feet, shaking in anger, and I was worried she was going to have a stroke. My heart went out to her, even though she was possibly the nastiest human being I'd ever met. It couldn't be easy trying to curry favor with someone your entire life, only to find out you'd been left out of the will entirely.

"You are correct, madam," the lawyer said.

"We will, of course, be contesting this will. It's obvious my father, God rest his soul, was insane. Who witnessed this travesty?" Robert asked.

The little lawyer pulled himself up to his full height again and glared at Robert.

"Reginald and my secretary. I took several steps to ensure my client's mental wellbeing before drawing this document up."

Bernie stirred in his bag right before the temperature in the room dropped several degrees. No one else seemed to notice, as they continued shouting and demanding action. I looked around, finally spotting Cornelius in the corner as I loosened the zipper on Bernie's bag. He looked sad and shook his head. Somehow, without his usual dour expression, he looked more human than he ever had. He made eye contact, and the pain I saw in his eyes made my heart catch. I had to do something, but what?

"Excuse me," I said, getting to my feet and waving off Zane's concerned look. "I didn't know your father well, but I know he wouldn't have wanted this."

Robert turned on me like a striking snake and I stepped back, alarmed.

"What do you know about it? Were you doing more than decorating this old pile? Were you warming his sheets and turning his mind against his loving family?"

Zane stepped in front of me, shielding me like a brick wall. I peeked around his shoulder.

"That's enough. Brynn has been subjected to witnessing a murder, countless pranks, and nothing but heartache from her brief association with this insane family. You're all a bunch of vipers, and you should be ashamed of yourselves."

Robert's eyes narrowed, and he said something incomprehensible before stalking out of the room. I saw Dave step back to allow him an exit and followed him. We'd planned for something like this to happen, and I could only hope everything went the way we wanted it to.

Cynthia was on her phone, gesturing wildly, glaring at me as I went past. I didn't want to know what she was saying and increased my pace.

I looked at Mimi and Reginald, who had their heads together. Mimi was clutching his arm and crying while he tried to soothe her.

"Robert, wait," I called, hoping I wasn't making a colossal mistake.

My footsteps echoed through the dining room before I found Robert pacing in front of the entry. He zeroed in on me and headed in my direction. I planted my feet and hoped our plan would work.

17

*R*obert approached me with an apologetic grin on his face, with his hands spread wide. I'd expected him to go on the offensive, especially with what he'd just said in the den, but once again, the members of this family surprised me.

"I'm so sorry. I don't know what came over me. Understand this is such a shock. I didn't mean to imply there was something going on between you and my father. Obviously, if there had been, you would've been the beneficiary, not some charity," he said, breaking into laughter at his feeble attempt at a joke.

Even though he'd arranged his face into a pleasant expression, his laugh seemed forced. I kept my face neutral as I searched my mind for something to say. Somehow, saying don't worry about it didn't feel right. I settled for a shrug.

"It happens. I followed you to assure you I met your father only a few days ago, and I'm here solely at the request of the sheriff."

Now was not the time to mention his father hired me to do more than rearrange some furniture and paintings. I smiled, hoping it came out genuine and not how I was feeling inside.

He clapped me on the shoulder, hard, and I stumbled back a step, eyes narrowed.

"Thanks for not taking offense. You're alright. You know, while I have you here, there's something up in the attic I'd like you to look at and give me your professional opinion, if you don't mind. It's not part of the estate if you're worried. I have a few things stored up there that I purchased with my money."

I hesitated, trying to make sense of his question.

"I guess I could look at it."

"It will just take a few minutes," he said, motioning for me to follow him. "I plan to sell it in town before we leave, but I want to make sure I get a good price on it."

I followed him warily, and we headed up the narrow staircase to the attic. His mood had changed abruptly from sheer anger to jovial, and I didn't know what to make of it. My instincts told me to go along with it, even though I was sure I was following a murder up to a secluded space. I shook my head as I got to the last step, remembering how other run-ins with murderous people had gone. Newsflash, not well.

Once we were in the open space, Robert spun around, obviously looking for something.

"Can you describe the piece?" I asked. "I've spent time up here and I might have seen it already."

"Oh, yeah. Good idea. It's a chest of drawers, about three feet high, with Oriental carvings."

I turned to my left and headed towards the windows.

"I think I saw something like that over here."

He followed behind me and I pointed to the black lacquer chest I'd seen. The ornate carvings were painted with crimson and orange, but faded with age. I'd noticed it before, appreciating the art déco piece, and wondered what it was doing up here.

"Yes, that's it. What do you think of it? Is it worth anything?"

I tapped my finger on my lip and quickly did some calculations in my head. It was nice, but there weren't many people interested in chests like this. I shrugged and turned to face him.

"I'd say around fifteen hundred to two thousand dollars."

His face fell and his shoulders slumped, and he looked suddenly older than the fifty-ish I'd pegged him to be.

"I see. Sorry to waste your time."

"No worries. I'm sorry if it's worth less than you thought. The market for something like this is pretty small. It's a beautiful piece, though."

He snorted, and I turned to leave. He put a hand on my arm to stop me.

"We don't have to rush back down there. I think I might have something else up here for you to look at."

My hackles went up, and I backed away, desperate to put some space between us.

"I really should go," I said, edging towards the stairs. "There's an antique store in Creekside that could probably be of more help. I deal with a lot of antiques, but the woman who owns the store is an expert. She might even have some buyers in mind for you."

"That would be great. I'll tell you, finding you've been cut out of your father's will, after years of expecting something different, really makes you take stock of your finances."

He looked so dejected, my heart softened a fraction, and I doubted my theory that he was the killer.

"I'm sure it's rough. I'm sorry things didn't turn out the way you'd hoped."

"You can say that again," he said, pacing in front of the windows. "Not even the bloody house. What's Reginald going to do, put it on the market? Over a hundred years of our family's history for sale? My great-grandfather built this house, you know. It's only ever had Graffs in it."

I didn't dare tell him I was completely aware of Cornelius' role in the place, so I remained noncommittal. He obviously wanted to talk to someone, and if he was the killer, I needed to stick with our plan and try to get him to confess.

"I see. That's got to be hard. That's probably what will happen, though. Everything in the house will most likely be auctioned off."

"All these memories. Well, with any luck I can get the old man declared legally unfit, and we won't have to worry about it. It's an added complication I wasn't expecting, but I guess that's the next step."

"Added complication?" I asked, turning to face him.

Robert's face tightened, and he stood up straighter, squaring his shoulders.

"I mean, on top of having to deal with things like the funeral and such."

I felt a chill on my skin as the temperature in the attic dipped, but resisted the urge to look around. I had a feeling Stephen was close to confessing. What had Mary Helen said? Something about the house knowing in its bones when something bad was about to happen. While I didn't like to assign feelings to inanimate objects, I couldn't deny something had shifted.

"You know, there's something I wanted to ask you, but with everything that's happened, it slipped my mind. When you were talking with the Sheriff, you mentioned having a conversation with your father. Something about him making odd financial decisions. What was that about?"

Robert's nose flared and his eyes took on an unfriendly cast as he looked at me.

"I don't see how that's any of your concern," he said, moving towards me.

I walked behind the chaise where Bernie had been lying, feeling more confident with a physical barrier between Robert and me.

"I was just thinking you said you were afraid he was going senile. If that's true, that will probably help you with overturning the will. Maybe you can have the courts go back to the old version."

He brightened and nodded his head.

"You're right. Thank you for that. I'd almost forgotten. Father had recently divested some of our assets into cash and I didn't think it was a smart decision."

An icy chill went down my back and I heard Cornelius right behind me.

"He's lying again. They argued over who was going to control things. Robert wanted to invest in cryptocurrency, whatever that is, and Stephen told him that was a silly idea. Robert spent all of his money and he wanted to dip his dirty fingers into the family funds for himself," Cornelius said, whispering in my ear.

Robert was looking at me strangely while I listened to the ghost and I smiled and nodded, hoping he'd think I was just slow.

"I see. Many people don't believe in cryptocurrency, it's a tough sell."

I waited to see how he'd react, and I wasn't disappointed.

"Exactly. I'm glad you understand..." he said before trailing off and a new light shone in his eyes. "How did you?"

"I have my sources," I said as I walked towards the stairs again, wishing I'd waited until I was closer to drop my little bomb.

The cold deepened as I passed by Cornelius. The ghost's face was full of righteous anger, and his eyes were blazing.

"He's the one," Cornelius said. "I'll get help. Keep him talking."

"That was a private conversation. Are you spying on this family? Trying to blackmail us?"

"What would there be to blackmail you over?" I asked. "Or are you referring to the fact you killed your father when he wouldn't give you what you wanted?"

"You don't know what you're talking about," he said, spitting his words. "I'm innocent."

I stopped, facing him full on, feeling I was close to getting him to confess.

"I think I know, though. I think you argued with your father. I think during your little sojourn, while everyone was in the den, you went to your father's office and saw the new will. You'd been planning something for a while though, hadn't you? Your finances are a wreck, and you needed help. Help your father wasn't willing to give. When you found out he'd written you out of the will, you lost it. You went to the kitchen and put something in your father's drink before Reginald picked it up. You hoped since he'd been named the executor, everyone would blame him, didn't you?"

He looked shell shocked as I talked, and his red face slowly paled.

"I don't know what you're talking about. You're mad."

"That's a favorite excuse for you, isn't it? Reginald saw you leaving the kitchen, but he didn't want to throw you under the bus since he's fiercely loyal to this family for some unknown reason. I'm not the only one who's figured it out, Robert. Eventually, the truth is going to come out. The sheriff already knows what poison killed your father. It's only a matter of time. You'd be better off admitting your guilt and plea bargaining so you don't get the death penalty."

"I can't plead guilty. Do you know what would happen to someone like me in prison? They can't prove anything! I made sure of it."

He paused, breathing hard.

"Robert, it's done. The game is up."

His eyes narrowed, and he started moving towards me again. I looked behind me, seeing the narrow staircase was almost within reach. It was a mistake. He was in front of me by the time I turned back.

"I don't think so, little Nancy Drew. You're the only one who knows. Have you ever heard the story of my great grandmother? The poor thing fell to her death, down a flight of stairs. These old houses have the most rickety staircases, don't they? I think history might just have to repeat itself."

He didn't know how right he was. I prayed Cornelius had found Bernie, and that Zane and the Sheriff were close as I squared my shoulders.

"I have heard that. Her son killed her. Guess you're just following in the family footsteps, huh?"

A wicked feminine laugh filled the attic and Robert went completely white as he looked around.

"What was that?"

"I believe you were talking about your great grandmother's unfortunate demise. Would you like to meet her?"

He backed away from me, looking around the room like a cornered animal. An icy breeze twisted around my body, ruffling my hair. I kept my eyes on Robert, watching his every move. He opened

138

his mouth several times as the laugh grew louder, but nothing came out. Finally, he stuttered, shaking as he put his hands up to his head to cover his ears.

"Stop this. What are you, some kind of witch? What are you doing? Look, we can work out a deal. I'll get my father's money and I'll pay you to keep your mouth shut. Just stop whatever it is you're doing. No one has to know what I did. We can keep it between us, okay?"

"I'm afraid that won't be possible," Dave said from behind Robert, snapping his handcuffs on Robert. "You're under arrest for the murder of Stephen Graff."

He read Robert his rights while Zane and Bernie came up the stairs behind me. Zane crushed me into a hug and I buried my face in his chest. The temperature warmed up, and I finally stopped shaking as my adrenaline spike petered out.

"Thank God you're alright," Zane said. "That was the worst half hour of my life."

"You're telling me."

Bernie wound his way around my ankles and I bent to scoop him up, nuzzling the fur on his neck.

"You're never using yourself as bait again. I can't believe I agreed to this. You don't know how hard it was to sit still, knowing you were potentially in danger. This little guy got out of his bag and yowled like the biggest cat you've ever heard before, streaking out of the den. I followed him and Reginald took Dave up the back steps."

"I'm glad Cornelius was here or it might have gone really wrong," I said, voice muffled by black cat hair.

Bernie chirped and leaned into me, whispering.

"I would've known even if he wasn't here," he said. "We're connected, you and I."

"Brynn, I've heard enough to get him charged, but can you stop by the station later to give your full statement?" Dave asked.

I nodded, noticing Robert was staring at Bernie.

"See! She is a witch. She has a black cat and everything," Robert said, spit flying. "She put me under a spell and made me confess to something I didn't do."

Dave rolled his eyes and marched Robert towards the back stairs, Reginald in tow. The elderly butler stopped and nodded at me, smiling, before following the pair. I took a cleansing breath and shook off the residue of the fear I could still feel clinging around me.

"Well, at least we got a confession," I said.

"I wonder what will happen now," Zane said, taking me in his arms again. "Seriously, we're never doing this again, though. If someone has to be bait, it has to be me."

"Well, in a perfect world, we'd never have to think about being bait again. That just sounds so weird."

"You're telling me. Are you ready to get out of here?"

"Past ready. What do you say we go grab a bite to eat? I've still got some work to do here, but I think it can wait until tomorrow."

Zane grinned and threw his head back in a laugh.

"Only you could be hungry after going through something like that."

I shoved him gently and smiled, elated we'd cracked the case. I shifted Bernie in my arms and led Zane down the narrow stairs, blanching a little as I realized how close I'd come to going down the stairs completely differently.

"Speaking of food," Bernie said, "I'd like to remind you I require more sustenance than the average cat."

"I know. You're anything but average, buddy. Thanks for saving my tail. Again."

He kneaded my arm as we walked outside. I took a deep breath and looked up into the blue sky, grateful I was alive to appreciate it. Zane curled his arm around us and we headed towards the Jeep. I took another look at the house as we pulled away, and promised myself that I'd help Mary Helen and Cornelius solve their differences and, hopefully, move on to a better place.

18

he next morning found me looking up at the Graff house, hoping that this was the last time I'd ever have to set eyes on it. I'd spent the rest of the previous day being pampered by Zane, and making sure Dave had everything he needed to lock Robert up for a very long time. The man was still raving about me being a witch and part of me felt he was hoping to get an insanity plea. Heck, given the state of this family, it was entirely possible they were all bonkers. Bernie sat at my feet, tail wrapped firmly around his little feet.

"Well, buddy. Are you ready to see if we can help Cornelius and Mary Helen?"

"That's why we're here. Let's get a move on. The faster we're done here, the quicker we can go home."

"No kidding. And to think, a few days ago, I was moaning about not having anything to do."

"That'll teach you."

The doors swung open, revealing Reginald, his white pompadour higher than I'd ever seen it.

"Miss Brynn! And your lovely cat. I wasn't sure if I would see you again after yesterday's kerfuffle."

I giggled at his word choice as he ushered me into the entryway. The place seemed calm, a state that felt entirely unfamiliar.

"Where is everyone?"

"The Graffs have decamped, for now at least. Stephen, the younger, asked me to pass along his regards, if I were to see you. The rest, well, I won't pass along *their* remarks."

"That's probably a good thing," I said, spotting Bernie's bag by the table at the door. "Oh, thank you for finding that. I totally forgot to grab it when we left yesterday."

"I put it here just in case you came back. I'm so glad you did. Mimi will be thrilled you're here."

"How did everything end up?"

He frowned and shook his head.

"Cynthia is doing her best to see how to have the will overturned, and she'll probably win. She's got the best lawyers in the state working on it. Mimi and I are to remain here, for a few weeks at least, while we look for alternative lodging. As for Robert, you probably know more than I."

My heart went out to the elderly man, cast out into the world after a lifetime of work, with not much to show for it. I'd had a feeling if the will was overturned, Cynthia would make sure he didn't see a dime, and I'd put a plan into action. I couldn't wait to tell him about it, but held my tongue for now.

"He's probably going to spend the rest of his life in prison. I feel bad for his children and wife. It sounds like he squandered away all their money."

"I'm sure Cynthia will make sure they're taken care of. Well, I hope so anyway. She's good friends with Lucinda."

I nodded and looked around the house before turning back to Reginald.

"Would it be alright if I went into the den? I have a few things I'd like to do, if that's okay."

He nodded, seeming to understand what I meant. He cleared his throat and adjusted his collar.

"Will you need any help?"

I shook my head and put my hand on his arm.

"I don't think so, but I appreciate the offer. It shouldn't take me too long. I'll let you know as soon as I'm done."

His face cleared, and he ushered me into the den, watching as Bernie trotted after me.

"He's a magnificent cat. And so well trained. I'll leave you to your, well, whatever it is you do."

I bit my tongue, knowing exactly what was going through Bernie's mind at that moment.

"Thank you," I said as he left the room. "Okay, Bernie. Let's see if we can do this."

He rolled his eyes and fluffed up his fur.

"I'm not worried about it. Hush. I need to focus."

A familiar chill crept up my arms as Cornelius slowly manifested in front of us. I wasn't positive, but it seemed like the dour man was actually happy to see us.

"I trust everything turned out satisfactorily?" he asked, pulling his chin up.

"It did. I appreciate your help," I said, matching his formal tone.

"I did what I could before I couldn't hold on anymore. I'm glad to see you weathered the experience."

"That makes two of us. Cornelius, there are a few things I'd like to talk about, if you don't mind."

His eyes softened, and he nodded his head.

"If you're here to offer to assist me in passing to the other side, I'm ready to try. I find I've grown tired of this place. Whatever happens to the house is none of my concern. Not anymore."

I glanced at Bernie, and he closed his eyes, ready for step two of our plan.

"That's wonderful. There's something else I'd like to do, though."

"Really? What's that?"

A soft, musical laugh filled the room and Cornelius's eyes grew wide as his wife, Mary Helen, materialized next to him.

"How?"

"Well, that's a fine greeting, you old stick," she said, drawling her words. "You and I are going to have words, cat. I don't appreciate being dragged here against my will."

I held up my hands, wanting to forestall a fight between the two ghosts before they could hear me out. Bernie stalked in front of me and sat down, ears stretched high.

"Say what you want. This has been a long time coming. Now, be quiet and let Brynn talk."

The two ghosts goggled at Bernie, and I resisted the urge to smile. My haughty cat certainly put them in their place, and I took advantage of their momentary silence.

"What he means to say is I think there are some ancient misunderstandings that need to be cleared up. Mary Helen, I appreciate your help yesterday, and your guidance. Without you, I don't know if I would have put the pieces together."

She preened, tucking her bobbed hair behind an ear. Cornelius harrumphed and tensed his jaw.

"I don't know about that," he said.

"Both of you played a vital role in solving Stephen's murder, but that's not the only murder that happened in this house. Mary Helen, do you have anything to say?"

She looked like a schoolgirl as she kicked at the floor, studying her feet. I raised an eyebrow at her and folded my arms over my chest.

"Fine. I didn't kill you, Corny. I never would've hurt you. I found out who did, though, and once I knew, the same person killed me. I think you know who it was."

His face softened as he searched her eyes.

"You don't mean..."

"I do. It was our son. I'm sorry. I didn't know what he was going to do. I honestly thought you'd eaten something and died from it. It wasn't until later that I put the pieces together. By then, it was too late."

"Why didn't you let me talk to you? All these years, I've been chasing you around this house."

She looked into his eyes, and her tough facade melted away.

"I don't know, Corny. You know how I am. I always loved games. Once I started, it appeared I couldn't stop. You were always so easy to tease. Still are."

I thought he was going to erupt, but he surprised me once again. He threw back his head and laughed. Hard.

"Oh chicken, I always appreciated your spirit."

Bernie and I made eye contact as I mouthed the word 'chicken' to him and he gave a little kitty shrug. These people were something else.

"It's too late to get justice for your deaths, but at least you both know the truth now," I said after a few minutes of listening to them reminisce. "Would you like to leave this place and go on to a happier one now?"

Cornelius turned to me and nodded sharply. He took Mary Helen's hand in his and steeled himself.

"I'm ready. How about you?"

All three of us looked at Mary Helen, and she made a face as she saw us staring at her. It would break my heart if she refused to follow Cornelius into the afterlife. It was obvious, despite their flaws, they loved each other, even after all this time. I crossed my fingers as I waited for her to speak.

She finally let out another laugh and shrugged.

"Heck, why not? I'm always up for an adventure."

Bernie nodded at me and closed his eyes. I followed suit and soon felt a warmth overtake my body. I cracked open an eye and saw bright light streaming behind the couple. They turned around and their faces seemed young again as they looked at it in awe.

"Is this it?" Cornelius asked, looking over his shoulder.

"It is. You're ready."

He straightened and looked at me, all traces of his sourness gone.

"Thank you, young lady. I know I was rude to you, and for that, I'm truly sorry. I knew you had gumption, though, and you've proved it ten times over. You helped heal this broken family."

I nodded, to overcome with emotion to speak. This moment was always so emotional for me. Cornelius and his wife had been trapped here for decades, and now they were finally going to their true home. The light became brighter and a feeling of love washed over me.

They walked, hand in hand, towards the light. Mary Helen stopped and turned towards me, her features hard to make out in the brightness.

"Tell Old Charlie he should come join us. We'll have one heck of a party for him when he does."

My laughter mixed with tears as she wiggled her fingers at me in a wave, and they slowly disappeared. I took a shuddering breath and wiped my eyes as the light faded and normalcy returned.

"And that's that," Bernie said, stretching. "Let's go home."

I scooped him up in my arms, not ready to speak just yet, full of happiness that Cornelius and Mary Helen had found their love after all this time. I met Reginald as I walked through the dining room, and he gave me an uncertain smile.

"Did everything... work out?"

"It did. You shouldn't hear any more footsteps or feel any more strange drafts."

His face cleared, and he produced a wrapped package from behind his back.

"Mimi asked me to give this to you. She said you were a big fan of the roast beef."

Bernie sniffed the package as I took it from the butler.

"Thank you so much. I hope everything works out for you two."

He straightened and turned, leading me to the front door.

"Everything happens for a reason, I always say. I trust that somehow, we'll land on our feet."

"It was a pleasure meeting you and your wife, Reginald."

"I feel the same way. If you ever need anything, I'm only a phone call away. I know Mimi and I would like to stay in the area, but if we can't, I'll let you know."

"Please do. Thank you for everything."

He surprised me by giving me a big hug and grinning before opening the door for us and handing me Bernie's bag. Bernie sniffed, and I slung it over my shoulder, figuring he'd rather I carried him.

"Drive safely."

I walked back outside to my car, happiness bolstering my steps. I'd talked with Zane the night before and we'd hatched a plan to help the butler and his wife. Once I was in the car and the roast beef was safely stashed where Bernie couldn't get to it, I called my friend Bob Tremaine, who'd put this whole adventure into motion.

I hit the hand's free button on my steering wheel as I drove down the drive and got onto the highway.

"Bob Tremaine speaking."

"Hi, Bob. It's Brynn Sullivan. I wanted to thank you for the referral to Stephen Graff."

"I heard about that. I can't believe he's gone. I hope you're okay and everything got figured out?"

"It did. Listen, I've got an idea I wanted to run by you. I recently came into a little money, but I don't feel comfortable keeping it. Do you know of any homes in the area that are for sale? I'm looking for something nice for an older couple. A fixer upper would be perfect."

Zane and I wanted to invest the check Stephen Graff had given me into a small house for the butler and his wife. Logan had already agreed to do any needed renovations for free, and I was going to make sure the inside was as nice as possible. Somehow, it felt like the right thing to do. I waited for Bob's response, hoping he had something available.

"I have a few properties that might fit the bill. Would you like to look at them? I can make time later today."

"Sure. Just text me the address for one and I can meet you there whenever you're free."

"Before you hang up, I have another referral for you," he said, voice dropping.

I looked over at Bernie and his ears perked up.

"I'm listening," I said, trying to ignore the feeling of dread creeping up my spine.

"Well, you know the old Maddison House, right?"

I did. The Maddison House was one of Deadwood's most popular haunted attractions, and it was actually haunted. I'd been to the

147

popular tourist spot a few times and met some of the resident ghosts when I was a kid. They were all friendly, so I wasn't sure where Bob meant.

"I do. What's wrong?"

"Well, um, I don't know how to put it into words, but I guess things have, well, changed there. Something's going on. The owner called me this morning, wanting to know if he could sell it. He wasn't himself. Would you be willing to visit there next week? I need to firm up a time with the owner."

Bernie caught my eye and nodded his little head. I sighed, wondering what I was getting myself into.

"Of course. We can talk about it more when you show me these houses."

"I've got time in half an hour. I'll send over the first address. See you soon."

I signed off and shook my head.

"Do I even want to know what this is about?"

"Probably not, but hey, at least our lives are never boring. That's a nice thing you're doing for Reginald and Mimi, by the way. I'm proud of you."

I straightened in my seat, my heart full at his praise. I stroked his black head and thought about how much my life had changed recently. I wasn't sure what we were going to run into on our next adventure, but I knew we'd meet any challenge together.

DON'T MISS THE ETHER IN THE ENTRYWAY!

What happens when a popular haunted mansion becomes a little *too* haunted?

The historic Maddison House has always been known for its ghosts, but suddenly, something changed, and this tourist attraction is about to go off the rails. The workers are terrified to return, and the ghostly residents want some answers.

Brynn and her wonder-cat Bernie are on the case, but this time, they may get more than they bargained for!

Get your copy now!

BOOKS BY COURTNEY MCFARLIN

The ABCs of Seeing Ghosts

The Demon in the Den

The Ether in the Entryway

The Fright in the Family Room

The Ghoul in the Garage

The Haunting in the Hallway

The Imp at the Ice Rink - Spring 2023

HAVE YOU READ THE RAZZY CAT COZY MYSTERY SERIES?

The Body in the Park
A Razzy Cat Cozy Mystery

"I'm a cat lover and read many cat mysteries. Courtney McFarlin's Razzy Cat Cozy Mystery Series is my favorite."

She's found an unlikely consultant to help solve the crime. But this speaking pet might just prove purr-fect...

Hannah Murphy yearns for a real news story. But after a strange migraine results in an unexpected ability to talk to her cat, she must keep the kitty-communication skills a secret if she wants to advance from fluff pieces to covering felonies. And when she literally trips over a slain body, she's shocked her feline companion is the best partner to crack the case.

Convinced she's finally got her big break, Hannah quickly runs afoul of a handsome detective and his poor opinion of interfering reporters. And when she discovers the victim's penchant for embezzlement and fraud, she may need more than a furry friend and a cantankerous cop to avoid ending up in the obits.

Can Hannah catch a killer before her career and her life are dead and buried?

The Body in the Park is the delightful first book in the Razzy Cat cozy mystery series. If you like clever sleuths, light banter, and talking animals, then you'll love Courtney McFarlin's hilarious whodunit.

More reader comments: "The Razzy Cat series is a joy to read! I have read the first three, and just bought the fourth. These books are well written, engaging stories. I love the positive and supportive relationships depicted amongst the main characters and the cats. That is so refreshing to read. I look forward to more books in this series. I will also be reading some this author's other works. Well done, and keep writing!" - Ingrid

Buy *The Body in the Park* for the long arm of the paw today!

Keep reading for a sneak peek at Chapter One.

BONUS: CHAPTER ONE OF THE BODY IN THE PARK

Friday, June 19th

The hum of the newsroom refused to fade into the background as I worked to file my last story for the day. I'd been assigned a fluff piece, which I usually hated, but considering it was almost the weekend, I wouldn't complain too much. I was looking forward to two blissful days off and some quality time away from work.

I've been working at the paper here in Golden Hills, Colorado, for two years, ever since I graduated from the local college. I'm originally from a tiny town in South Dakota, and I love living so close to the mountains. I'd discovered a love of hiking while I was in college, and I couldn't imagine leaving to go back home to the family farm. There's nothing wrong with farming, we all gotta eat, but for me, I needed mountains and adventure.

I read through my story one more time, checking for errors, stopping to admire my byline. Hannah Murphy, that's me. Seeing my name in print never got old. I hit enter on my laptop, posting my story to my editor with plenty of time to spare on my deadline. I rummaged around under my desk, looking for my purse. With any luck, I'd be able to slip away a bit early and head home. I poked my head over my cubicle and looked over at the glass office where my editor, Tom Anderson, was banging away on his computer. I stifled a laugh. Tom was old school, from a time when the clerical girls typed everything on typewriters, and he resented being forced to use a computer.

I grabbed my things and headed down three cubicles to where my best friend, Ashley Wilson, worked. Ashley was my roommate in college, and we were both journalism majors. While she lived for the lifestyle pages, I was drawn to the hard news and wanted to make a name for myself as a reporter. I wasn't kidding myself. I knew it was a miracle our little newspaper had its doors open still. Most small newspapers had folded years ago, and it was tough for an independent outfit to keep the lights on. But I was hoping with some luck, perseverance, and hard work, I'd be able to move up the ranks to a serious news position.

I tapped on the wall of Ashley's cubicle and flopped into the chair across from her desk.

"Hey, Ash, you about done for the day?"

Her tongue was poking out from between her lips as she focused on her screen, ignoring me. I leaned over to see what was engrossing her and saw she was working on an image in Photoshop. Since we were such a small paper, most of us had to do our design work for our stories, which wasn't always fun.

I watched her as she worked, admiring her long brown hair that was impossibly straight and glossy. My hand went up to my unruly nest of blonde locks, and I gave a rueful smile. No matter how often I tried to straighten my hair, it never turned out as pretty as hers.

We were complete opposites. She was tall, statuesque, and dark, while I was short, thin, and fair. She enjoyed shopping and partying, while I was an outdoors kind of girl. It didn't matter, though. I'd never had a friend as close as her. She gave a little shout and hit save, turning to face me.

"Hey Hannah, sorry about that. The image didn't want to cooperate."

"No worries, been there, done that. What are your plans for tonight? Are you hanging out with Bill, or was it Will?"

"Will. He was also three guys ago. You gotta keep up, girl!"

"Sorry, are you hanging out with what's his face tonight?"

"I was unless you wanted to do something. We need a girl's night out."

"We do, but not tonight. I think I've got a migraine coming on. I'll just go home and hang out with my cat."

Ashley made a sad face and heaved a sigh.

"That's how it starts. You're in your twenties, and you spend a Friday night alone, with just a cat for company. Before I know it, you'll be my crazy cat lady friend who becomes a shut-in and only leaves to buy more cat food."

"Wow, that's a depressing and strangely detailed future look."

"I call them as I see them. I kid, Hannah. You should get out more, though," Ashley said, giving me a look.

"I know, I'm just not a peopley person. I enjoy being outside, not cramped in a loud bar with sweaty people being all, I don't know, sweaty. I like my cat. I like quiet."

"I need to find you a man. I think Will had a brother..."

"Thanks, but no thanks. I don't want to get set-up with a cast-off's brother. That would be even sadder than being home alone with my cat. Seriously though, have fun tonight. I expect a play-by-play tomorrow."

Her phone rang, cutting off our conversation. I waved as I grabbed my bag to leave. It looked like the coast was clear, so I headed towards the door, determined to make a break for it. I wasn't lying to Ashley, my head was pounding, and I wanted to get home and change into my jammies.

"Hannah! Wait!"

I groaned when I heard Tom's voice, turning in my tracks to head back to his office. I stopped in the doorway.

"Hi, Tom. How was my article? Does it need any edits?"

"It was fine. You self-edit well. That's not why I wanted to talk to you," Tom said, gesturing for me to come in and take a seat.

I plopped in the comfy chair across from his desk.

"What's up?"

The way Tom dressed was as old school as the way he typed. His button-down shirt was turned up at the cuffs, exposing a myriad of ink stains. He had a nice face, utterly at odds with his gruff voice. He scrubbed his bald head and leaned back in his chair. He looked at me closely for a beat.

"Hannah, you've been doing a great job lately. I know fluff pieces aren't what you want to do, and I appreciate you've been good about working on them. I can tell you put the effort in, even though you don't enjoy the subject."

"Thanks, Tom, that's nice of you to say."

"I'd like to try you out on a few tougher pieces. The next big story that breaks is yours."

"Are you serious? I'd love to try some harder news pieces!"

This was the most exciting thing to happen to me in months. I was finally going to sink my teeth into some meaty stories!

"That and whatever else you can dig up. I know you're young, but I think you deserve a shot."

"Thank you so much. I won't let you down."

"See that you don't."

With that, he waved me off and turned back to his computer, cursing under his breath as he started banging on the keys again.

I floated out of his office, almost forgetting my headache. I got to the parking lot and climbed into my ancient Chevy Blazer. I'd saved up my money back in high school, and it was old back then. It'd seen me through college, though, and with any luck, it would get me through until I could make enough money to replace it.

Traffic was picking up as I navigated my way back to my apartment. Golden Hills was growing fast, but I was lucky enough to find a place that backed right onto a huge green space. I had acres and acres of wilderness to explore via the trail that led to the Crimson Corral park. It wasn't cheap, but it was worth it to have an outdoor space and a killer view.

I trudged up to the top floor, feeling my headache get worse with every step. By the time I made it to my door, I was feeling odd. I walked in and immediately tripped over my cat, Razzy. I'd had her for two years, ever since I got my place. I scooped her up and cuddled her close, apologizing for tripping over her. She was a Ragdoll cat, and I had no idea how a beautiful, purebred cat like her had ended up in an animal shelter.

Her soft fur felt like a rabbit, and her little purrs made me smile. She was a quiet cat who rarely meowed. I put her down and walked to the kitchen, trying to decide what to make for supper. A quick check of the fridge revealed I needed to do some serious grocery shopping. As I stood in front of my cabinets, a wave of nausea and dizziness rushed through my body. I gripped the counter to keep from falling over.

Razzy meowed at me, cocking her head to the side. It was like she could tell something was wrong. I skipped dinner and walked back to my bedroom, holding my head. I changed into my favorite pair of fuzzy pajama pants and a tank top. Maybe if I just lay down for a few minutes, I'd feel better. I collapsed onto the bed, and Razzy jumped up next to me, snuggling close. Closing my eyes, I felt darkness rush towards me.

* * *

"Mama? Mama!"

A small voice pulled me from the darkness. I blinked open my eyes, trying to get my bearings. I felt grass underneath my feet. I looked around and realized I was in a park. My stomach felt hollow as I looked around, trying to figure out why I was outside. I glanced down and saw I was still wearing my fuzzy pants and smiled. This must be a dream. At least, in my dream, I didn't have my headache.

"Mama?"

There was that voice again. I looked through the gloom, trying to see if a child was wandering around. This was a strange dream for sure.

"Mama! There you are."

A small figure walked towards me and sat in front of me, looking up into my face. It took me a second to recognize my cat, Razzy, sitting there. Her whiskers bristled in the faint light from the moon.

"Say something, Mama. You're scaring me. Why are you outside?"

I felt my world rock as I realized Razzy was talking to me. Like, really talking. I laughed when I remembered I was dreaming. Geez, this was one crazy dream. I shrugged and went with it.

"Razzy, what are you doing in my dream?"

"Um, I'm pretty sure you're not dreaming. I followed you out of the apartment. You left the door open, which isn't safe, by the way. I tracked you here and kept calling you until I found you. Why didn't you answer me?"

Ok, this was weird. She was talking to me like she was a human, and I could understand everything she was saying. This had to be the winner for my strangest dream ever.

"You were calling for mama. I figured there was a little kid in my dream who was looking for their mother. I didn't know it was you."

"I always call you that. To me, you are my mama," Razzy said, her eyes rounding with concern. "This is weird, though. I always try to talk to you, but it's like you can't understand me. Why are you suddenly understanding what I say?"

"Must be the dream. I'm sure I'm going to wake up any second and find you cuddled up next to me."

"You're not dreaming, but whatever. Can we go home now? It's getting cold."

Razzy fluffed up her fur and turned to her left, looking at me expectantly. Her tail curled into a question mark as I stood there, staring at her. Well, maybe if I followed her, I'd wake up. I must have had something bad for lunch.

I shrugged and followed her.

"Lead on, MacDuff," I said, as I fell in behind her.

"It's actually 'Lay on, MacDuff,'" Razzy said with a sniff. "Humans, always misquoting things."

"Wait, you know Shakespeare?"

"I know way more than you might think."

I couldn't help but laugh. I had a talking cat who was also a literary critic in this dream. I needed to write this down when I woke up.

Razzy paused, her tail going stiff and then curling down behind her. Her hackles went up, and she sniffed the air.

"Stop, there's something up ahead."

"Are we going to meet a talking dog next? That would be pretty cool."

I moved past her, ready to get out of this dream and wake up back in my apartment. I took a few more steps and fell over something stretched across the sidewalk. As I felt around to see what I'd tripped over, my hand came in contact with something cold and squishy. With a little shriek, I scooted back. This dream had taken a disturbing turn.

I felt in the pocket of my pajama pants and grabbed my cellphone. Switching on the flashlight app, I held it out in front of me, my hands shaking. I wasn't sure I wanted to see what it illuminated.

There, next to me on the ground, was the body of a man. I placed my fingers on his neck and felt nothing there. Jumping up, I screamed, convinced now was the perfect time for me to wake up. I looked over at Razzy. She walked closer, sat down, and shook her head.

"I told you, you're not dreaming. You should probably call the cops."

Realization flooded through me as I took stock of the situation. My feet were freezing on the cold concrete. I checked my arms and noticed I had goosebumps. I pinched myself and winced when I clearly felt it.

Razzy walked over to my feet and gently bit down on the top of my foot.

"Ouch! Why did you do that?" I asked, rubbing my foot.

"You didn't seem to believe me you're awake. You were pinching yourself, so I thought it would help if I pitched in too." She gave what I assumed to be the cat version of a shrug. "Call the cops."

I hesitated for a second before numbly obeying her suggestion and punching 9-1-1 in on my phone.

Get your copy now to read the rest!

A NOTE FROM COURTNEY

Thank you for taking the time to read this novella. If you enjoyed the book, please take a few minutes to leave a review. As an independent author, I appreciate the help!

If you'd like to be first in line to hear about new books as they are released, don't forget to sign up for my newsletter. Click here to sign up! https://bit.ly/2H8BSef

A LITTLE ABOUT ME

Courtney McFarlin currently lives in the Black Hills of South Dakota with her fiancé and their two cats.

Find out more about her books at:
www.booksbycourtney.com

Follow Courtney on Social Media:

https://twitter.com/booksbycourtney

https://www.instagram.com/courtneymcfarlin/

https://www.facebook.com/booksbycourtneym

Made in the USA
Monee, IL
27 November 2024

71453014R00099